Eternal Bliss

A Rhyming Romance Novel

By

Stéphane Parker

Imperative Publishing
Detroit, MI

For more information, email:
ParkerRomance@ParkerRomance.com or Follow @ParkerRomance

©2013 by Stéphane Parker

ISBN 13: 978-1-4675-7290-3
Published by Imperative Publishing, LLC Detroit
Printed in the United States
Book design by Stéphane Parker

ACKNOWLEDGEMENTS

Here we are again. It's been several years since the releasing of Eternal Kiss, the world's first and only true rhyming romance novel, and I'd like to thank God for my expressive talent as I understand more than ever than I'm responsible for the sharing of my gifts. I'd like to thank my parents Carlos and Sharon Parker for believing in my writing talent and helping me stay focused when my mind was centered on a million other things. Momma, you told me to concentrate on my writing and that's what I'm doing. Dad, you stay strong and we will play one more game of basketball together.

Mike, my brother, man, you know your brother is all over the place sometimes and I love that we've never had a fight. We don't always hang but I know that you have my back and I have yours. Whatever you choose to do, you know I'm with you. Auntie, man oh man, this one may be too hot for you but I know you'll buy one, or two, or maybe 10. I love you so much. You call me Christopher just like Grandma did and you always seem to be there to bail me out of something. I appreciate you. Uncle Rusty, I'll keep on keeping on. I was made to find a way or make a way; it's just that fire in me. Jae and Ash, what can I say, we have to keep on laughing. I have memories that will forever remain present. I love y'all.

To Jerome Rutledge, Dre' Clark, Darryl Holmes, I'm with y'all for all time. I see us becoming men and I know others recognize that as well. Let's keep being role models.

Shenee' Davis and Rhea Lewis, and Dwayne Mitchell I believe in y'all and I know y'all on the cusp and as the lyrics of Journey state, don't stop believing.

My acknowledgements are few this go 'round as so they should be. I love passionately and Sarah Phinnessee receives that passionate love. Baby, you helped solidify the second half of this book. Your passion created those words. I love you.

And you, the reader, thank you for you continued support and encouragement because I know y'all have been waiting for the sequel. It's the most endearing, erotic, and sensual writing I could muster at the time. Enjoy my creative rendition of making love. Eternal Bliss is here.

Lol "Do it for the kids..." The story is definitely not for children's sensitive ears. ~ Lauren J.

That damn near made me come - but it gave me the inspiration, as well. Thank you, sir. ~ Christina W.

Keeping it on point my guy. You're still raw and wild as ever. Much love. ~ Terrance T.

The idea of being in love is something people don't admit to freely and I am glad you decided to do that. It is important in my opinion when that is done because then it means you recognize things about yourself and are not afraid of emotions which leads to the true connection interally, which is priceless. ~ Jarrod. J.

You're utterly genius in every way. You're amazing. I love this story. ~ Yolande I.

So... I think I'm exhausted after reading that! lol. This had a fluidity to it that is somewhat unlike anything I've ever read. I'm quite intrigued. It kept pulling me in and making me read it. I couldn't pull away. I look forward to the conclusion. ~ Alexis G.

I swear if I didn't know any better I'd think you were schizophrenic or something....The essence of the words feels as if it's really written from that person's point of view...you know how you can write something from another point of view but it's obvious that it's written your way...Yea you don't have that blockade....Straight, raw emotion is what flows from your pen....I admire that. ~ George T.

You never fail to make me want to read more. God has blessed you indeed with a truly expressive mind. This is your calling. ~ Kyle B.

I am.....in love with this one. OMG. ~ Tia C.

This is inspired writing. Nicely done. Gina L.

You inspire me to wanna write with a passion that I sense from your words. ~ Reggie D.

Your creativity is just astounding. Well done. ~ Faith J.

Ste'phane, I love this ...makes me wanna just hold my bae...and kiss him softly, and... you know. ((smiling)) Give him that Eternal Bliss. ~ LaToya M.

Beautiful. ~ LaRhonda R.

Although I rarely comment it's not because it isn't great work. I don't comment out of humility brother. Your hard work is taking you further. Continue to grow brother. I'm enjoying every minute of it. ~ Lamar P.

You may be ahead of our time. Don't let anyone or anything slow you down. O. Randall

WOW!!!!! Eternal Bliss touched me on a very deep level. You are the man. ~ Wanda L.

Whoa!!!!!!!! Damn Steph, ... you have just left a man of many words speechless! I began reading it ... I ended up watching it! Hell, at one point I became him ... you made me him ... because of how well you tell it, it not only draws the reader in but it envelops and surrounds them ... and there is no room for the reader anymore. We're forced to be one of the characters as the story unfolds! Damn man. How in the hell did you do this? ~ Michael S.

Wonderfully loving book.... truly takes you into a passionate multitude of lifetimes of lovers. Excellent Book ;-) ~ Leandrea H.

Fire, brother, fire, ~ Devon M.

AWESOMELY written. ~ Simoan R.

I don't have the vocabulary to express myself as well as I'd like to; so I'll just say that I love your Eternal Stories. Yes!!! ~ Timika T.

YOUR VOCABULARY IS SICK; WHICH YOU KNOW I MEAN SICK IN A GOOD WAY! YOU ARE REALLY A MAD GENIUS!! ~ Ashley C.

As I'm reading, I am realizing what a gifted writer you are; to be able to have the reader feel what you're feeling/writing, to go on the journey you've laid out on paper... that's a real gift. I love your love lines (you arrange things we've heard/read before in a way that's not "corny" or cliché but indeed genuine) and your eroticism is titillating! Continued blessings to you and yours. ~ Cheryl B.

I loved this. The way you broke this down was like a grown-up Dr. Seuss mini love story. I found myself reading and I couldn't stop because I wanted to see what was next. Not sure how you pulled me in like that, but I think it was the way you broke up the sentences/syntax, the rhyming scheme... All in all, I enjoyed it. Nice one Ste'phane. ~ Nicole W.

For tonight, we will be the ingredients used to make a grand love
Let every eye and mind recognize our expression as pure, this is not
lust

You press your finger to my lips to shush my whispers

You open my bedroom door, we shall bask in delight
I tip toe pass you and you close the door, everything feels so right

Will you make the son shine within the layers of the night?

I ease close to you and enjoy the proximity of our souls
We breathe in the same air; I can feel that you want to lose control

Your eyes are full of sultry desire, a volcanic type fire
I ask "How high are we going tonight?" you answer, "Higher than the highest higher"

Is that right?

You walk away from the door trailing your hand across my chest
Night's light is seeping into the room; our eyes capture sights of glimmering flesh

You glow just like an angel

I follow you around to the bed, staying behind you closely
I align my arms around your waist; your warmth is what I crave for mostly

We gaze at the moon and see the stars twinkling brightly
Oh how much fun we've had sailing and navigating the night's seas

Tonight... we'll fly once again but this time... without our wings

You turn to me and rub my face as if for the first time
You examine my jaw line and lips; tonight will be our first time...

Well, at least in this life on Earth that... we'll make love

I can feel the wanting and the yearning of your flesh as I caress your arms
Our silent room is blaring with emotion; our intentions hear the exotic alarm

It's time... it's time to awaken to a new day of pleasure

We agree without moving a muscle

And

We agree without blinking an eye

We agree without the smallest hint of struggle

And

We agree because every angel has already nodded from the skies

Yes... it is our time

Guidance is unspoken yet we innately follow our soul's direction
We've always found ourselves together; we're drawn to the other's affection

And... without accident...

You glance at to the bed, hold my hands, and lower us to the sheets
Our sparks produce a fire of eroticism as we intend to birth true love within the
heat

You lean in and kiss me and all of the visions return
Every inch of your magnificence will receive my utmost concern

The room whirls...

Fast

Your tongue twirls...

Faster

I'm falling back in love...

Faster

The bite of your love bug...

Fast

Tonight, we've experienced the sensations of an Eternal Kiss
Tonight, we'll experience the sensations of an Eternal Bliss

Because yes... it is definitely our time

Come into my room... give in to the moon

Step with me, step into my suite, Love, my loving room
It'll be reminiscent of our future in Jamaica, in each past life; I've been your
groom

Never forget that and with that implied through my stare...

Your soft oatmeal skin absorbs my tender touch
We've landed within the bed and the room glows with a hint of Love's lust

The walls will speak of their memories from watching us

The walls will talk of our eternal sexcapades, the smell of our satisfaction
Of how our legs and arms reached up in attempts to find some type of aerial
traction

We arrange explicit words through our eyes
We've been the illuminating trail seen throughout the skies

Our defenses fall by our sides... You await the son's rise

Your artistic fingers trace the rim of my mouth; I hold your lower back
We lower back, there's no holding back; we are wheels set to a golden track

We sink further into the bed; we sink further into each other
We're warmed by June's heat as our arms become our covers

*I simply and affectionately love you... I exhale mental breaths of
adoration*

Since Earth has been a white, green, and blue ball, this is what I recall
You've left me in awe; you are my gravity and that's why I'll always fall

I'll love you through the ups and downs of scales and carry your every weight

I'll always fall for you

I'll out wait Patience for a chance to savor your Texas Tea's taste

I'll always fall for you

Since the start, I've always fallen for you
The echoes of my every desire's sound have stayed calling for you...

And it's mainly because you're Beauty's genesis

I've felt the heaviest aroma sit on my mind

It's because you have the densest scent

You've held residency in my every state of mind, you epitomize what's fine
Your silhouette's mist has been bottled for wine; you intoxicate the seconds of
time

4

The remnants of your uniqueness date back to a time before dates

To a time before hate, to a time...

Where desires manifested instantaneously, a time where dreams didn't wait

You've been...

The cadence of heart beats, the Isis that irises see
The essence of a pleasing breeze, the origin of attraction that birthed galaxies

You're the first sublime design, my gravity, I'm awed, you are the genesis of Beauty

And... You've kept us a part...

A part of the stature of a statue of art
I know that when you read my mind you appreciate my heart

You flash a smile because you can read the vibrations of my thoughts

I ease you onto my lap... I start to undress your attire of desire

Your tongue rolls kisses like tires
These sensations tap my intangible body like invisible wires

Record my chord's accord of how you mimic and resemble the Lord

Your breath hits my ears... "Ahhh"

Your appealing voice causes me to swell
Your depthless gift awaits me and I shall delve

You bashfully smile and reposition yourself even closer
This picture perfect evening is set to hang as the photo of every lover's poster

I rub your ears and make sure they are attuned to my passionate speech
I make sure your eyes reflect my heat, this will be a night were two souls meet

Yet...

It'll be a night where one spirit will remain, the spirit of love
The same and identical love that has shielded our warrior hearts from above

I pull you close and kiss your neck

Your perfume raids my nose like an army swooping on sleeping enemies
The scent throws my mind into another place; you hold my back with hands full of energy

Your scent reminds me of a flavorful breeze and...

I can't just simply explain what I feel for you
How my silky, threading soul spools and spills for you

But...

I can kiss you into fantasies and awaken you into dreams
I can surround you with the love of a man that can provide every needed mean

Nothing ever bestowed before my being rings a scream...

Of allure, pleasure, love, honesty... and...

Passion like of what your tongue sings

Within infinity is an infinity of infinites
There is no possibility that another soul shares your mended scent...

Besides me

The way your lips curve, the way your reign bows and arches
You're mathematically and architecturally a masterpiece, you're why Spring steadily marches

And

I can't just simply explain what I feel for you
You can't simply say you can't feel me too, you know that I'll kneel for you

But know this

I'll truly let go of the wheel if what we willed is through
Just don't be surprised at what runs besides my side is as red as the passion I feel
for you, what spills is you

*I pull your shoes off, I remove your powder blue tank top... it falls
to the floor*

I hear your heart; the sound resembles a harp
Your hands trace my face down to my inner thighs like they're reading a Braille
chart

You finally blink... I comprehend and exhale

It was envisioned in your pair of eyes, that this paradise was dared to rise
It's because we're paired to strive, as a union wholly, and holy spirits established
our care for life

In no way could a slow pace diminish the speed our soul's race
We're on a path that strolls straight; we've loved as lovers throughout all time
since we were taught how to fold space

We've ironed out every wrinkle in time

My pulse increases, the noise of my mind ceases
Your words enter my eyes; I see your perfect lines like they're Navy pant creases

I can recall...

Your hair has been thick and curly, short and wavy, even bald and smooth
Yet never has your attractiveness been branded to your braids or locks, your
beauty permeates social truths

You present presents in dynamic fashion whether you're clothed or naked
Debonair and stylish, only elation leaves your mouth on the days and nights I'm
feeling rakish

And... I tend to exude my flair like that everyday

I'm yearning... yearning for your...

Cocoa brown skin

Honey glazed lips

Cinnamon glares and strawberry flair

Your chocolaty graspable hips

Tonight will be deliberate... this will not be a coincidence... You call my name... "Baby" and...

You ease off my white polo; your weight still rests on my legs
Our emotions heighten as I watch your bra fall from my palmed ledge

I savor the softness of your breast; I yearn for your caress
Genuineness melts within my kiss, I further tongue tattoos to your neck

I suck your breast and glide my tongue around your nipples
My tapping's rapping and lapping await the shore of your beach's bliss; it wants to swim within your trickle

I hear your mental vibrations... you speak to my mind

The warmth of us emblazes the scenery; we're being covered by a loving fire
You fulfill my desires; soak me with kisses until I start to perspire

Or shall I say leak... and...

It's not at all from this June heat
You enjoy my neck and fancy yourself with finally having me atop your sheets

Your body will sing in high pitches, my hair will stand on end to applaud
I'll open my mouth widely as I'll attempt to put all of you into my jaws

I want you to...

Cup my breast in your hands with the delicacy you'd have toward a rare jewel
I want you to feel every curve of my desire; I want you to taste me growing hot when I try to stay cool

You reach within my mouth and introduce a kiss to my thirst
I'm holding your masculine heart despite the fact that you're still wearing your t-shirt

You push me deeper into stimulation; you hold my attention like a hand
You lean in further with this French translation, your diction is grand

8

You lip my mouth the lyrics of rhythm, my whole existence sways as if...

You are bowing to me with the salutation of your waving tongue
The glow from your aura is immense, intense, your devotion is felt and it's as heavy as a ton

You watch as I remove your clothes as we stand... my feminine touch...

Raises your t-shirt above your head, I admire your chest
I slowly unbuckle your belt and unbutton your shorts with finesse

My praline and cream kisses melt within your warm mouth
I want you to spoon with my double scoops of breast all over the house

You step out of your shoes and let your shorts cover them
I capture your eyes while I enticingly run my finger along your boxer's rim

I pull them off and kneel before my king
My lips, tongue, and mouth act as a passionately elite team

I tease your crown with long, soft draping touches of my lipped gown
I hold your handle as I part my oral gates and then lower them down

You grab me and...

Stand me to position me atop the covers; I release onslaughts of my kiss
Your stomach's skin feeds my hungry touch, the sensation, intense

You lean me over and the mattress conforms to my back
This is the most beautiful creation on earth, that is a fact

My tongue crosses your stimulated chest like muscle striations
Your face blushes, my nipples erect, areolas flush, your pupils are dilating

Everything that makes you manly opens me up

You run your hands from my arm pits down to my awaiting waist and hips
This motion mimics the movement of your pottery when you molded the vase to implant why we exist

And... that's to become one...

Tonight, we plan to...

Move more fluently than under water troupes of ballerinas
Our action never needed choreography, only the readiness of the lenses of those
who have seen us

Label us enslaved to trust

You toss my feet straight into the air, you handle my sole
You spread my legs while your licking takes a Southern stroll

You glimpse into my spirit and I know with your biting your lip...

You've dreamt of removing the veil to Heaven and now you hold it
You've allowed me to control it, and now I've allow you to unclothe it

Our desires yell... the room hears... Silence

Nothing can be heard, thoughts can't form sounds into words
Everything existing besides our smiles is blurred, Time's speech is slurred

You open your third eye and take over

Masculine energy helps me see that...

Your name can't accurately describe you nor can any amounted price tag measure
your worth
Electricity can't light more lamps than the way you light up eyes with the energy
your smile exerts

No title can justify your position in my life

No love poem could or would ever be more beautiful, more sacred, more
endearing than you
Calculators can't make two, one, nor can they make one, two, like you do

Your words are the seeds responsible for the blooming love I have for you in my
heart
Your actions were the bulbs that illuminated the path when I was blind and
stumbled through the dark

Slowly... yet ever so slowly...

You've blurred memories from the past to seem like the present
Your etched pictograms lay as fossils of divinity; you've made kings of peasants

Your anticipation approaches me with caution; you're shy in your natural state
My heroic touch assures you I feel a similar way, we're sharing a natural fate

We're naked

We embrace each other like once lost but newly found lovers

How long can we make tonight last, what if this was our last tonight
Let me kiss your entire foot and sole, let your soul feel every kiss, no matter how light

And know that...

I'll do the right breast exactly as I'll do the left
We'll go until there's no screams left, know that tonight wouldn't dare go left

This night... tonight...

Will write us right

Within the layers of the night...

This plight will fly as high as heavenly flights destined for delight

Shine for this sun

I'll cover your full moon with palms as soft as midnight clouds

Snarl and growl, bark and howl

My animalistic instincts have always encouraged me to eat you out

How long can we make tonight last, what if this was our last tonight
I'd use my might to kill time and stand tall in your vagina with a Giant's type height

Feel this bean stalk bring orgasmic fantasies to life tonight
The hype, your pie in the sky is why I dive; it's why I'm feeling so alive

I've traveled through space and time to kiss your face and grind
Patience's divine, she's allowed me to witness your grace as mine, you add depth
to the pace's climb

The universe respects that we've previously made time stop
You'll moan until this son's last light has shown, and if the night cap could pop...

We'd go on into the Sun

Know that we could never cease as in our ending could never be
Our heir could never leave because the lungs of our break-up will never breathe

So how long can we make tonight last, what if this was our last tonight
Let me hold my breath and imagine your permanent smile, never let your hand
flash goodbye

I kiss you in the hollow spot between your shoulder and chest
You ease and looked into my soul, your body is screaming, yes, yes, yes

Yes!!!

I whisper love themes with lips covered by the glaze of honeyed moons
I send shivers up and down your spine, as my belly dances, your tummy swoons

I lick and taste across the stretch of your chocolate temple of grace
Predicting your smoking hotness, I look forward to feeling the erotic vapors
massage my face

I can't control it...

My skin crawls towards you; this will be this life's first time
Let this be our birth rhyme, the catacombs of our Jones will be explored when we
search minds

This night will allow us to...

Sweep and leap about the other like ballerinas at Julliard
This is who we are, Beauty's art and I'm destined to play my duly part

Tonight... I'll prove that...

Despite all geographical evidence stating our location; every time I kiss you, I
know I'm home

Tonight... I'll prove that...

No matter the distance we're separated, every time I imagine your face, I'm no
longer alone

Your landscape has been perfected through the articulation of the universe's
imagination
To attain the height of your persuasive power is the only reason I've vied for
aviation

Tonight... I'll prove that...

I'll love you more than physically, more than mentally
I'll love you spiritually because your angelic grace was sent to me

I'll awaken your slumbering orgasms from their sleep
We're going to make love between the covers as I've described in my poetic
sheets

Look into me

Open your heart and welcome me home
Trace my mouth with your finger tips, instead of making love, let's make a poem

I love that you've founded 'We' and grounded me
You have the name that all ears need to hear me yell from the mountain peaks

Love, I'm in love, Love

Aerial stretches of cumulus clouds will always crowd around when we produce
thunderous sounds

And

We've painted walls with hurricane flames until views through window frames
showed chocolate fish drenched in a pool that'll never leave us drowned

We are strange imagery

Your question breaks my thoughts

"Do you know how much I love you?" I listen and pause
The way you rub my eyebrows implies that of your soul, you want to give me your
all

The light sprinkle of your deepest emotions touch me
You explain how your character's figure was drawn for none but me

Your eyes' survey fills my blank expression

I'm hearing what your peering speaks, I'm paying attention
I'm spending seconds to afford the luxury of what you'll mention

Your gaze speaks and admits...

Your love for me runs as deep as the Heavens are high
As long as eternity can reach is the length of time my face has stayed in your
mind's eye

I know how much you love me

Your breasts become spouts letting your flavor quench my thirst
Scratching, clawing, smacking and slapping, tonight, won't hurt

While my licks cause your calm reserve to shed
I have your freshly shaved legs sprawled across the bed

You...

Feel my suede soft touch smooth over your ebony velvet skin

You...

Feel my guided fingers gingerly tickle your expectance to a grin

As romantically as the ebbing waves hugs the shore
That's identical to how I'll manage to hug yours...

Yours meaning...

Your lips, each of my precise kisses will be calculated

Yours meaning...

Your eyes, each sensation will have them dilating

The one in your mind as well

I've always seen you

Stirring my mind until I'm dazed and imagining...
You grabbing me, performing acts outlandishly, endless pampering

Your stare screams your plans of coming hard, I'll swallow it
Be my Coke shaped Brandy and I'll hold you with a tight alcoholic type bottle grip

And... I can feel it...

Our sexual expectations coast on brain waves glowing as bright as a flamed sage
It appears a plain stage but this bed will provide the path to our famed ways

Tonight, we will shine like... like... super stars

The silk sheets have awaited a sexual performance quite patiently
You control my hands over your curves, passionately pacing me

I position myself between your legs and raise your left foot to my mouth
I extract the essence of you from your soul; I ease each toe in and out

I believe you are poetry... and...

If I could use your body parts as lines of my poems
I'd use your breast in twisting tight word play to tease them, but I wouldn't show
them

I'd...

Use your lips to ensure that each metaphor is graciously kissed
I'd pen out your hips as similes to accentuate their beauty which cannot be missed

Would you allow me to use you vagina as my message, I get that deep
Your eyes would be my flash of intelligence; we'd raid the dreams of all who sleep

I'd...

Use your tongue to spread spring; you'd speak life to everyone hearing
I'd stack my rhymes to jingle as wind chimes to mimic your earlobe and earrings

Your kissable feet

Would be the tone of my poems, smooth and soft
The tonality of your assurance would be how I ended my flow, no analogy would
be lost

You're worth it

You're more than the worth of life
I'd die to prove my love, you, rhythmic poetry, you're my wife

Throughout all rhymes, throughout all time

We're involved in the breaking of Earthly laws, but, this is Elation's cause
This love we share is untainted, undiluted, and completely unflawed

And since I believe you are Poetry... and because...

It's a certain rhythmic breathing being created; we're becoming a uni-verse
Your galaxy spins around me, astoundingly we travel astral seas and we seduce
and swoon the Earth

The atmosphere sweeps your delicious scent across the globe
You wear my body as your robe as we stroll and ride down the smoothness of
Love Making road

The mysterious magnetism of the Moon Queen is kissed by the son
Even before the rising, we both had shone but had never shun, this is how angels
have fun

Always remember that...

Even Astrology knows... I've told every world of every time that...

You're a gem in eyes; your prose opens the poetic locks
It's lovely how your seductive voice in movement can stop mental clocks

You've frozen time with me while tip toeing that taboo line
You've pulled the inhibitions from my psyche at light speed, our stare cases will
always wind...

And...

Create the double helix of a new passionate scene's DNA
You exhale faith and breathe in fate; your solace is seen in shapes

You're

You're an artist of expression who loses herself in her own gift and talent

You're

You soak further into brain tissue as people realize that your wish is granted

You're totally and fully aware and appreciative of your Queendom
You're retarded with metaphor and imagery and help illiterate eyes not to seem dumb

And it's because...

You speak to third ears, you manufacture word spears
You swallow the worst fears as you know that the most ungrounded mouths thirst tears

You'll never see her weak

Despite the time she's baring her insecurities...
Witness angelicness at it most heavenly, it's most quintessential purity

You truly make me feel invincible...I feel that...

It's not a stone structure of rhyme that I can't flow down

And

Not a palace of precise passages portraying perfection that I can't own now

I have enough cash sense to buy every house sitting on every writer's block in every mind
I have an infinite river of oceanic mechanics that seas excellence every time

It's you that I owe my gift to... Angel...

Never could I ever forget the feathers that fell from your endeavors
You're the heir of the nicest weather that severs the clouds of the nay-sayers' never

I'll love you for an eternity for that... never forget that...

Yesterday I ran for an opportunity to have you in my life
Today I run for the opportunity to have you as my wife

Tomorrow, I'll run for the opportunity to keep you elated

And

I'll continue to run for your excitement until Gravity's impatience makes us
weightless

And... we float like...

Confetti in the wind of celebration

And we float like...

Your mind's thoughts during penetration, or your moans when my tongue makes
your heartbeat hasten

You're the inspiration that stirs decision making, risk taking
You became the gist of mysticism that resulted from wishes mating

Never could I ever forget the feathers that fell from your endeavors
You're an improved better, a pure, pristine, realized dream the instant you've met
her

Or you and you...

Speak with passion; your heart's furnace has learned this
Knowledge is responsibility and your sensitivity towards the mimicry of love is
honest and earnest

Your mental strength only alludes; I sense your unconscious hints
I felt your help, you relieved my mind and though one's life time flew in sprints...

The moment we really owned is indelible... it's...

A magnificent, inerasable molasses of attraction...
Trapped in infinite fractions of marvel that is partial perfection within the limits of the vocabulary of the masses

Ineffable

You were, you are, you will always be my angel

And...

I was always, I am always, I will always continue to thank you, thank you

Thank you

And I'll forever tell every world of every time that...

You move with limbs as nimble as palm trees
Your kisses light up worlds like the opening sentence of Dawn's speech

Your sex appeal's fluidity is why the seas movement cease
No prudence seeps, you could make Monogamy's tutor cheat

Wow

You're as delicate as cotton roses, Gentle's child
You surf brain waves and invades subconscious space covering millions of mental miles

Per visit

Woman...

Your passion springs forth from the oasis of greatness
Your elegance streams through your motions and your soul is heard in your statements

Your body of water holds buried treasures that the smartest of pirates couldn't fathom

And

Even the most acute of visionaries couldn't imagine the worth of your mint's lather

My tongue's combination of swirls and twirls around your pearl notices your
jewelry box is open
Your ocean is golden; it unfolds and consumes my stroking

Now... once again, I've awaken

You were designed to construct the archetypes of dreams
You comprehend with a chronologic that figured out why the river of Time
streams

It pools and collects, of that, you totally respect

Your power resides in the gift of making destitute depths of desire un-less
A tongue-less, lung-less, speaking breath of fresh air that's done, less

While making love...

You're an ever on-going, flowing, glowing moment
You're the essence of the miss's mist that I'm holding; you're why I'll stay golden

And if anyone else needs to know

I fell in love with a mind in a realm that doesn't recognize gravity
It's because of your soul that Argyle galaxies' diamond patterns shine so lavishly

You spread verbose on my toast and sprinkle hyperbole on my eggs
You flip imagery over the edge and bleed passion until every line is read

You...

Arrange paradoxical metaphors into simile's that make sense
You help me resuscitate a dilapidated great mess into greatness

You're my imagination in the flesh; I surf in its wake
My dreams curse when I wake, and Lady Luck flirts in the skirts that you've made

You've also made me understand that...

I'm the producer of Word Play; I sink or swim with its articulation
A verbal chauvinist's creation, this is the beginning of me making me in the
making

Your breasts bestow the bountifulness of infinity
If my affinity toward your femininity contained any more energy...

Then...

We would've actually glowed when we entered this room
You're the melody of my tune, you're why I'll never see ruin

Our lips touch again... the world hushes... you whisper to my thoughts...

Husband...

Angelic sculptors have chiseled your existence into my lungs
I breathe the monologues of your spirit; I shall always repeat them in our native tongue

You've depicted my silence's resilience within the strands of the multiverse
Within the uni-verse, rhymes of your medicinal metaphors halt the hurt...

Because essentially... we can only create perfection

We're the strongest union to ever unionize, we've hued the skies
We soothe the vibes; our raw love is able to be seen by the most nude of eyes

You know that I am...

A black woman with intelligence, I've birthed the filament within the gents

That I've...

Birthed suns from lungs that have been in hell and now they've exhaled innocence

That I've...

Mothered nature, crystallized air vapors

That I've...

Been depicted as the eclectic genius, Venus and I don't have a genus

That I've...

Reigned within the rain of shame and tears of pain, I'm the life maker

That I've...

Quilted moral structures of ethics into cement being a hieroglyphic seamstress

That I'm...

The most sought after trophy when celebrity isn't enough for glory

That I'm...

No-thing to possess, there's no place for me on the highest shelf

That I'm...

The originator of seduction, the moral to his-story

And that...

You could accumulate a million worlds of wealth and that wouldn't be a tenth of my self

Since...

My thoughts were draped in locks of onyx, my tongue has been silk
My body was cast from gold and my breasts pour out divine milk

My eyes are diamonds and I had a platinum sheath for a hymen
You know the price of the protected, only you can comprehend the finding

Of all things... you know that this is...

Just a sample of who I really am and what I'm truly capable of
You've discovered the flesh of Fantasy by showing me unconditional love

I'll never, ever forget...

Throughout the life of every world we've occupied...

I've felt you swim an eternity of laps as I waved my sea on your lap

My love...

You've been the engineer laying the steel track within my vaginal tract, you've provided the warmth of its insulated wrap

I slid and swerved you hors d'oeuvres of my curves, never once did you deem it absurd
You've sampled my creamy candle and I've handled your trophy with a skill reserved only for you to observe

We've become what we thought we'd always become since the day we became... that's the strangest secret

And now your masculinity takes over

Within this kiss, I fall through time to an earlier us... I stated back then that...

You're beautiful, exclusive, truly one of a kind
You possess an exuberance that equals the sun's shine, you constantly pause minds

When you smile...

My heart skips a beat; your style is quite unique
It's quiet when you speak; you are intentionally and intellectually deep

Know that...

Rain clouds dare not to dim your radiance
You're passionate as can be; you duplicate what sun rays emit

You lift everyone to your height... not physically, but emotionally and spiritually...

You're...

The pulse of an upbeat existence, you're a studious young lady
You can make an insane person heavily stricken with psychosis not seem so crazy

And today... you're still everything I stated about you

Our matrimony shall carve out the diction of fairy tales
Our change shall affect every well, whimsical wishes know of us very well

Because...

We've ruled armies of Charm, see, we commanded weapons of mass instruction
We've gathered the faith of every fate and started the entrusting...

That with perseverance and persistence... anything can be done

You're heavenly...

Even an atheist would bless your body

You're immaculate...

Even Jealousy wouldn't break the camera that could possibly produce your copy

I further recall our past memories and speaking to my inner me...

I remember that I bathed her with every kiss I gave her
She pooled a delicate lake; you rode the waves and would wade with her

You both moved in unison, you heated her multiple orgasmic galaxies being a uni-sun
You both breathed and left bedrooms in ashes until eternity's tune was done

This has happened for as long as we can remember
The race was over before it started, since creation, she's been your winner

My winner... and because I'm owed you...

I'm owed your soul; I deserve to have the best of you
Though others may have taken the rest of you, I'm here to not just rescue you...

But to pull out the wrecks in you... To pull out the rest in you

We have to face and conquer your past to create your next today
I'm blessed to say that I only started to grow after I confessed the frayed

And...

That was with self, and you can do it too, with my help
Let your gracious tears fall, I'm certain that the fantasies will melt...

Into a now... so now and forever...

I'm here for you; I'm owed your soul
I give my spirit in return, I'm the one in which you can console

I slip my tongue into your mouth and I say...

For one night isn't enough to have you in my room
Understand that I was meant to love you since I've left my mother's womb

Read my signs; know which way my body will move
I'm going to show you just how much emotion can spill from our groove

Hear my entire message... and... temporarily leaving Heaven...

With my hands falling to your waist, you arch backwards to reveal the purest of pearls
I thumb your button as your hips and my finger synchronize into a series of swirls

You whisper slurs I can see, your volume is too loud not to feel

"Baby," calmly...

Your voice swims within the canals of my inner ears
You massage my mind with your ripples of passion and your power is clear

It's been evident that when your hands have touched the sides of my head
Your soul was sitting in my temples and praying to my spirit to be wed

Prayer does work...

I remember one of our weddings...

Everyone becomes silent; everyone grows anxious to see... You

Beads of sweat excitedly build into slight streams of anticipation
My clammy hands grip the sleeves of my suit, I've been patiently waiting

White and gold attire matches this theme completely... it's Perfect

I can hear the light yet enthusiastic chatter happening behind me
Today, I will allow the letters of L-O-V-E to redefine me

I hear the ritual's music; everyone here can feel my emotions
Your father walks proudly beside you, he tears Devotion's potion...

Appreciation

I peer down my groomsmen line, they're all witnessing history
Heaven has loaned Earth one of its finest angels, the same one of whom Wishes
speak

The bridesmaids are all glowing, they are all gorgeous
White and gold suits and dresses outline the alter for a noteworthy performance

You gracefully bestow your beauty upon every mind as you walk nearer
The church is hushed by your aura; ears can only envision what eyes can hear

Your body language speaks volumes... it speaks Love's dissertation

The gown you're wearing exquisitely accentuates your spirit
It's as though you're one drop of perfection that fell as diamonds were tearing

You are so unique

Photographers feverishly snap pictures; we all enjoy the shutter sounding lightning
show
The dazzling luminance of your ripened glow, you're the image that God's
writings show

Angel, my angel...

The mortals of the world desires know no better; they've yearned to hoard you
But your type of plant can't be cramped; only an honest soul can be awarded you

It's evident that how you place your feet upon the flower girl's evidence
You breathe in Forever's scent; you were made to walk on petals like they're
sediment

The arching ceiling of the church echoes the awe, mimics our eyebrows
I was told a goddess was to enter my life, I just had to wait until now

I've wanted...

Her to be strong, able to write the wrongs

I've wanted...

Her voice to soothe me and groove me to her songs

I've wanted...

Her demeanor's shine to never be dimmer than a jewel's glimmer

I've wanted...

Heaven to understand my plight and be gracious enough to lend her

And now... you've appeared just as I've imagined you

I turn to see the pastor smiling; he looks down to see me beaming
Is this happening as it's seeming, my best man subtly leans in...

"She is one beautiful woman... congratulations, man"

You're about half way to me, your magnetism is relentless
I'm not one for rushing a great thing but I'm looking forward to that sentence

You may kiss the bride

Your grin indicates our win, everyone stands to view you
Even the sleepless dreams knew you but still they rest their eyes to lie on you

The wish of little girls is right before them, so is my idol
We're merging into one person; my name will change your title

*Miss? Not with me... Together, we're a hit... quick memories of you
flash and...*

I recall our dates in the summer, the phone calls in the fall
How you arrested my thoughts, how I fell under Karmic law

What goes around flows around

This is why I've loved you unconditionally, why I've love you exclusively
This is why my rhythmic touch dances, why I've improved my newest me

27

This is why my hugs are saturated with love, my smiles full of truth
Why this son presents as perfect of skies as possible, forget the blues

I smile at you in present time as I recollect on your smiles in my mind

I think to myself of the first time I saw your mind
You vocalized through your eyes and I knew it would only be a matter of flying time...

From the thoughts of my "I'll" to how we spoke of our "We'll"

Oh, how much you've changed my life, I do owe you my soul
The better half of perfection is what you're reflecting; I do owe you my soul

I do

Being in your company has helped me deal with me
Your encouragement has enabled my liberation, my sixth sense is freed

I feel things more clearly now... as you continue to walk down the aisle...

You're moving closer, your father is 'cat swallowed the canary' proud
His daughter is being given away to the one that has bested the best of crowds

I look and see your mom nodding her head at me; I nod and wink my eye
The sheer magnificence of your vibe is magnified and exponentially growing in height

An awed face is shared by the stars in space

I'm glad that the heavens have relinquished their greatest secret
For those who have been genuinely seeking and sowing, an angel has reaped it

This day will photograph unforgettable memories to my mind
Photographers catch the ever present glint of heaven as they still time

I can't tell whether the bright flashes are from cameras or from connecting with your eyes

You approach the bridesmaids as your father holds your arm tightly
I don't ever want to let you go, I can't wait until the pastor knights me

I'll always be in shining armor to disregard your every distress

The organ chords quiet to a low murmur, the entire church is hushed
With a quick peak before your stop at the altar, I see that you've blushed

The pastor commands attention

What man here today gives away this bride?
Your father says he is and steps back, I then step up to your side

You're not behind me... I'm not in front of you...

Exactly where your better half deserves to be... by your side

We hold hands and gently squeeze, we both glow with affection
Within the house of the Lord we're protected, we're moved under guided direction

The pastor goes on to read from the bible, our picture is still being taken
History is being made and our ever conscious future is being awakened

Remembering...

Years and years ago when my days moved way too fast
You presented my senses with the option to grasp a new touch of class

Your subtleties made your beauty scream more loudly, you became my favorite sight
My every breath carried your description, everything about you was right...

Except you being single... and that's why I was made... to change that

Our pair of eyes became their own couple, they spoke before our mouths
Your smile, wow, all I wanted to know was when, where, why, who, and how

I asked myself...

When had you escaped from my fantasies to roam this Earth?

And...

Where have you hidden your wings, beings fly that are equivalent to your worth?

Why have you...

Left my desires and wishes to the whims of chance?

Who...

Are you, my love, tell me you're the better half of this man?

And I kept repeating... How could this be real? How could this be real?

I broke my paralysis by waving my hand, you mirrored my action
We were pulled by attraction; we answered the question though no one was asking

Do we believe in love at first sight? Yes, yes, we do and for anyone with a paint brush and easel...

Illustrate our intention, decipher our dedication
The myriad of hues will be true, our color is maturation

Outline our visage, what does our silhouette reveal
Tint each shade of our devotion, our portrait of Love is strong as steel

I've come to see that...

We're...

A volatile, versatile, version of vintage vernacular

We're ...

A derivative of variables of unknown values, we are quite spectacular

Our...

Swerving images of rhythmic love collide against mental rods and cones
We hide in poems but appear to be the one that's controlling and driving tones

So, Illustrator...

Dip us into your water paint, spread us into a shape
Configure the vigor we hold in our poetic figure into the number eight

Let us round the finite twilight until our palms are pawns

Until...

Our pen become the dawn that'll bring light to sights as poetic alms

Draw out my life and erase the blemishes of my timidness
Embellish my relentlessness and add direction to my rambling's endlessness

I've asked the Heavens a million questions... I've asked it to bring me...

Someone to love, someone in whom I could share cares
I'll provide the shoulder as my childish fingers would play in her hair

Heaven, bring me...

Someone that will challenge me, to feed the famished me
That magic woman that'll help make sure that we don't vanish "we"

I've asked to receive a genuine excitement... because...

I want to be honestely enthused about the upcoming holidays

Heaven, bring me...

Someone that'll require me to have her hand after I receive her father's praise

I want to build a hammock in our backyard so we can sleep in nature
Let's draw sexual conclusions from hypothetical situations without the paper

You're stepping towards me as well; don't think I'm just waiting
Can't you feel my heart beat, see how fast it's pacing?

I'll bring you...

Your greatest lover, this is my vow
My patience possesses a perfected power...

I'll stay through the part where the rest have quit and now...

Heaven has answered my pleas, your ocean of physical beauty is all I see
We've bonded through pondering; I'm all the heir you will ever need

From that day...

My eyes have studied your beauty, I've memorize your smile
I've wanted to know each chapter of your life; I want your secrets to fill my mental files

I've perused your smooth vocal grooves and I've read your articles of clothing
Your glance it's unmistakably the result of heaven and passion molding...

And that's scientifically notated

Your voice had awakened feelings that I thought would sleep forever
Whether it were in print or picture, what I see in you, my iris has never captured better

My wandering heart has lost the hurt; it's healed since I've realized you're real
Since you let me feel what you feel and now I want you to feel what I feel

Feel this blazing love

You've kept massaging my masculinity with your femininity
For infinity, our divinity is the reason we will always raid the others memories

As you look back at me at the altar, I wonder what you may be thinking... your glance speaks...

When you've looked at me, you've always seen me
Not just my sexiness, not my breast, how my curves blessed this dress, just, me

I love you for that

I've wanted you to see past the blush, past the lips that haunt your dreams
You've seen me and have seen yourself wholeheartedly as being my mighty king

I love you for that

You gotten around your fantasies and the stereotypes, you've never been blind
You've seen my mind, my thoughts, but you've never seen yourself being left
behind

And I love you for that... and you've seen that...

These gentle arms won't rope around your neck to choke your masculinity
They'll release your energy and sensitivity, so you can see your inner divinity

So...

When you've look at me, I honesty knew that you've truly seen me
Listen with your sight, I've screamed for someone to see, for you to see me

And you're the chosen one... and I love you for that

Pieces of my dreams have combined to form your face
Pieces of my heart have been magnetically attracted to your grace

The more I think of you the more I find reasons to commit
The more I hear you laugh the more I realize that we fit

The pieces of my poetry have received your official stamp
The pieces you've given me has caused the panes of my soul's windows to damp

Who would've fathomed that a phantom of Love's past...
Could presently arouse promiscuous cameras to repeatedly flash?

I know I didn't

You're amazing; I can't put you into words
Though I try, I can't accurately put my feelings for you in words

Accept my teary eyes as indication that my love for you will always pour

The pastor announces to the congregation that we've arranged to recite our own vows

I clear my throat and I fix my upon your awakening smile... the testosterone speaks...

Being separated cannot keep me away from you
I'm within every element that creates you; we'll always find a way to renew

We'll grow old exposing the inner child that lives inside until the death
You're why I quest; I'll declare the depths of my soul to you until the atmosphere is out of breath

So... understand...

My heart will sit on your finger; my soul will rest on yours
My trust will rest in my actions and my love will spring from my vocal chords

Don't fear the separation, whatever you do, don't trust my death as final
Love can't conclude and where we're heading, seconds won't be allowed to time you

You'll stay with me for an infinite now

I can't say that I've returned because I've been here all the while
We will reign across eternity within a sky of passion making love on every ninth cloud

Love me as you have and I'll continue to become your better lover
You've replicated Heaven in your actions; I'll always be your infinite lover

The pastor signals to you... you peer into my eyes back a million years... you state...

If I had to spell love...

I'd use all of your names' letters
I would rearrange your face into phonetic symbols but if I could somehow make love better...

I'd paste your grace within the stroke of my illustrations
I'd fossilize your patience; I'd exponentially magnify your greatness

If I had to spell love...

I wouldn't put 'U' and 'I' together
I'd use all of your names' letters, armor-all the paper for harsh weather

I'd write Webster and let him know that you've redefined love
You've realigned my heart to your hug and that your kiss could double for a drug

I'm as high as the atmosphere in heaven; your presence is a blessing
I'd try to freeze time so that we could share the eternity that rests within every
second

If I had to spell love...

I'd use only your names' letters to spell us
If I had to spell love, I'd simply write out trust

With the vows exchanged... the pastor asks if there is anyone that sees a problem with our union continuing...

Without a sound being made, the pastor proceeds to announcing us husband and wife... he says to me... "You may now kiss your bride"

Your hand reaches to my neck, my hands reach to your back
Everyone stands and all you can hear are gasps and camera flashes snap

Sharp bursts of light blind Time, our anxious lips finally connect...

I speak to your mind

If for forever I could only kiss your hand then I'd cherish your lips
If I could only hold your attention then I'd be gracious for your hips

If...

I could only buy time to be with you then I'd love my paycheck
If I could only swim to prove my feelings then know that I'll always stay wet

If...

I could only have your back then I'd take the burdens off of your shoulders
I can only see your inner child so technically you won't ever grow any older

If...

You could only read my poems and could never hear my voice...
I'd write my exact meanings in rhyme and provide you with the choice

You can either see me in the paper reams or your later dreams
Either way, out of all the subjects you'd see me as the greater king

And if...

I could only feel your touch when I closed my eyes
The hell with reality, I'd remain slain to slumber with you in my fantasy life

The Heavens...

Witness our consummation through the perfected lenses that tell and scope
Even from unfathomable elevations, they never look down on a love that yells of hope

Now, currently...

Each fiber of your skin acts as a live wire

Tonight's anticipation rings loudly

We'll answer the call of Desire's choir

Tonight's anticipation rings loudly

Your beloved hands touch, your beloved hands feel
Your beloved smile speaks, for thy wish will be my will

Through my stare, you allow my mental declaration... Since the birth of time...

This room, these four walls, this bed
This whole event was written a story type romance and tonight every chapter will be read

You've carefully placed me under cardiac arrest

And...

To your physical visage, every naturalist would attest

True beauty... you're simply and truly beautiful

If I lost my voice you would still see how my words yell for you
You can't imagine the crimes of my fantasies; how they're gelled to brain cells for you

Do you understand how you make my frame sail
I don't think you understand that Cupid aims well

Remember when I taught Cupid how to use that bow and arrow?

Your body was built for his arrow dynamics and for me to manage
To not be taken for granted and for this son to always tan it

See my objective tonight as a guarantee of your climax
You've understood my words my dear, now just lie back

And now my tongue smooths over your oatmeal pavement... and...

What I'm smelling is a sexual propellant
It raises my eyebrows and gets my energy sailing

We're engineering the mechanics of making love
As soon as our physical graces touched, our bodies shared an amazing blush

While kissing your eager mouth...

Twisting and bending like ampersands
My passionate fingers swam and no amphibian could possess damper hands

I lower

As my tongue cycles around your nipples like puddle ripples
Sweet, passionate love making will be our language, spoken lowly and ever so gentle

I look you into the eye and tell you

"I need your thighs surrounding my face tonight
I need time to savor your clitoris until your legs lose all of their might

I want you... I want you to be...

My dessert, ease your sweets to my face
Gently force feed me your taste; honestly, my tongue can no longer wait"

But baby, please...

Don't rush me, let me take my time with my touch
My accumulative graces will add up and I'll know exactly when you'll want our
positions to adjust

Your wide set hips house cinnamon lips
They invite my tongue tip to take an erotic trip

I nibble between the pucker of your lips, I examine your most feminine sector
I spread your flower as my tongue circles around its nectar

Slowly yet systematically circling your swirling slit
I whirl my tongue like twirling hips giving your so far denied pleasure pearl a kiss

And...

As I ease between your knees
I tongue dive until I'm as deep as 80 leagues

You comb my waves with pleasure stricken fingers
An oral solo without the singer, this is fantastic fantasy dream stuff

You control my head by holding my ears
You twist and turn as my tongue wheel, you precisely steer

My lips rotate around your clitoris like a rotisserie rack
You bite and lick the air, imagining that you're kissing me back

My mouth motivates you to moan

You rub my head as my lips kiss here and they kiss there
You squirm and giggle; the sensations are raising your hair

Your follicles act as antennas, they receive celestial instructions
You're aware of our broadcasted event; the hall of fame awaits our inductions

I tack tact to each lap that savors the springs of your vaginal tract
You relapse to infancy as if intentionally to whine and coo, you know God is a fact

Your cuffed ankles rest at the nape of my neck
You secrete sex; your clit feels my every slurp and peck

I feel you trembling; the sensation is vibrating your thick thighs
I deliver a passionate dissertation with my closed eyes

Your slick warm liquid runs like a drawing bath

Your warm liquid...

Strikes my tongue with the sweetness of syrupped lightning

Your warm liquid...

Introduces me to a width that of which I didn't think my mental smile could widen

Your warm liquid...

Sweeps over my lips and into my mouth as if it were a wind's draft

Of a sexual storm that was brewing in the distance... I recall that...

For years...

I've yearned for a lady of your caliber
I've searched with wide eyes and have scratched the days off of my calendar

And now... I've found her

You're voluptuous and you're curvaceous with all of your graces
I'm so very gracious to finally get you naked and to get to taste it

I promise that...

Nothing will be wasted

From the last ounce of wine

To the last sweat drop on your spine

I'll hold it as sacred

I am not faking... I promise that...

This moment our passion owns is our greatest

Our...

Kisses speak in tongues; our hands speak with gripping conversation

Our...

Rhythm is ardently pacing while my touch is contour tracing

Until...

I'm faced to face hidden places and my lips are on an oral vacation
Communicating directly with your clitoris, my presence keeps your body shaking

But...

When we make the room colorful like a kaleidoscope and our hips collide us both

Side to side...

I'll probe, and I'll dip and dive my pokes

My slow stroking in slow motion will add more depth to your ocean
You biting my Adam's apple while I'm holding your coconuts will seem to make us float and...

As the covers...

Wrap us into a cocoon of explicit and exotic performances
A metamorphosis from like to love happens without forcing it, this is pure devotion, it's...

Pleasure reciprocated... these marks of passion won't be able to be graded

You pull at my shoulder blades; you mumble passionate passage of pleasure lowly
Only my neck can decipher your speech as I construct my groove slowly

All I can figure it means is... YES

I grip a lock of your hair and deeply grind until you wince
I have your left leg bent; you let out a yell as I manage to deepen another quarter
inch

Your eyes are wide open, your mouth is wide open, my penis' slide's stroking
You've cried hoping that a lover would come and make the spell of every night
potent

Well... here I am

This chemist's wizardry of magic is exclusive to your body, to your mind, to your
soul
Every past hurt and disappointment has been tallied up, my love for you has paid
the toll

Echoes echo as the volume of eroticism bellows, bellows
Your mind is blew with deep, soulful trumpet blows of pumping while my kisses
trail slow

From your earlobe to your neck, from your neck to your chin
You're blanketed by me as if I'm the wind, you growl and groan as you feel the
chills heat every inch of your skin

Exclaim our love, baby... sing for me

Howl like a lonely wolf beneath a winter moon
You secrete lakes of leaks as your bending swoons, pleasure is sent in tunes, we
were meant since the big boom

Theorists debate our origin but we state that we've just always... been

All that I've held in my rhymes is for this time
You soundlessly squirm but I can hear all of your joyous pouring into my mind

The silence fills with the sound; my lips are meshing with yours
My affection is yours; I want your scent to seep from my ebony pores

I lower

Your fingers run over my hair, my lips peck on the rim of your lair
You allow my eager tongue to place specifically, prolifically gifted kisses that
share...

My concentrated love for you

I swallow your essence as it keeps me alive; the taste of it keeps me awake
If the ideal of perfection were made physical, it'd be your shape...

Your vagina's shape and I don't mean to be facetious... I'm serious

Tonight...

We'll do more than pump and grunt, moan and groan

You'll be my obsession

We'll melt as one; we'll be each other's clone

Let's prove we're products of an eternal meshing

Let's spin into cyclones of nice moans until we vibrate the right tune
Our bodies will hum a hymn when we cum a gem that reflects me and you

And that is... The pure light of us

The moon light sneaks peeks between the blinds from the sideline
This is the perfect setting, love sure did pick a fine time

I ease back but hear whimpers that hint that I should finish my dinner
So I dive back down and search for more creamy peppermint inside your York
center

My native tongue speak fluent French, clitorally communicating
As more light seeps, the room is slowly saturating

There can't be enough words to express how you make me feel
You're my every desire, dream, wish, and fantasy and you're real

You speak through your hands...

My black angel wrap me in your wings, holds me across the celestial

I rub my hands through your hair as you whisper 'I love you's' in my ear
Your skin is so smooth yet powerful, your magic fingers make my passion
reappear

You let the key dangle in front of me, I respect your patience
I lie baring all and present my lock, you are granted my graces, and I know you're
gracious

I roll you onto your back... as I lower

My kisses zigzag across your midsection like streams from a river
I deliver careful laps until you shiver, I command Chocolate Thunder like a
wizard

You spin me around

One head North, one South, we lay as parallel pleasers
I swallow your swollen extension, as your tongue trail her but I'm no teaser

Like your every other talent, you prove to also be a voracious eater

Easy then soft, deep and hard, I apply varying tension

I feel you lean in to lip my canal; your mouth is burning hot
We're like flames atop candle wax and I'm melting, I won't see how we could
stop

I must tongue pleasant shark tales of terror since you're scared stiff in my jaws
I guide your blind artist through the warm hall of my mall as he admires my
textured oral walls

And until...

The sea of sheets are wrecked, until the mattress is off set

Until...

You've gotten all you can get and I know that seconds of dessert is all set

We're secure in this bed until our heat raises us away
We'll lie as the text between the sheets of our sex, and you'll silently concur and
say...

"I want all of you... because I've agreed to give you all of me"... And remember...

As we've toasted to Dawn and Aurora, you've enjoyed the breakfast love making covered by my syrup
As my tongue follows the curving contour of your oar, my fingers prepare the waters to be stirred up

I engulf your erecting peninsula, not with ease, but with every intent to please
I've stood open mouthed awed while my hands encouraged your spirit to wildly run free

I've tasted your passion and have taken pride in knowing I'm the only one to erupt your volcano
I have abilities that have made my design incapable of refusing you, there's nothing you have that my body can't hold

I draw conclusions against the walls of my imagination
You're half heaven, fully angelic; you're the most perfect creation

My body was naturally made to fit in your hands, to be aware of your delicate touch
You're worth the most of the much, and what I say to attest to your masculinity will never be enough

I Feed you and...

Let my cream covered pearl ballet on top of your lipped dance floor
For my oral presentation, my dear, this is what your erection stands for

With a palm full of jewels and a mouth full of you
You widen your rule from lands of lips to the origin of drool

I love how your...

Tongue scales my slick walls not being scared to fall
I feel it jump around my warm spring, savoring my all

And

My throat soaks for your strokes, it coats from your escaping yolk
Maneuver my mouthy moat, feel how my surfing, cycling tongue floats

Around the sides, over the top, along the bottom of your shaft

You then take control... as a man should... you feel my desires

You slide from under me and now position me back on my back
The room spins as stars out of space, we start to relapse into a relapse

Baby,

Your resiliency has a royal brilliancy
You glint like a sheet of diamonds would atop the waves of a million seas

What you feel is me, what I feel is you
We'll end the night riding a climax that I don't think could ever be finished or
through

You know I pen rhymes and desperately want me to tattoo a poem on your heart
I ink and embed a lost city of words on your chest praying that the buried treasure
and my hands would never part

You gaze into my eyes and speed light years throughout an infinite soul
You can read my mind, you sat up and my attention was under her hold

You whisper slurs I can see, your volume is too loud not to feel
My body flushes with the steam of passionate chills

I mumble sentences being under such a wonderful spell, you exhale, expelling
your thoughts
Time and our desires fought, I'm hoping Time continues to crawl

Slow and deep breathing with seductive glances means that the water's warming
Firm grips on my interest means that you're completely ready for the sexual
touring

With careful placement...

You surround me like seduced clouds to the sun of a candid dawn
Now I come to finally penetrate the great walls of Babylon

I lend my piece of a dream to your valley's pristine stream
The benevolence of our passion wafts as our bodies raft through a heavenly scene

You grab my arm; only on Earth does a love like this hurt a bit
I cup your breast; know forever that this is also where my heart will sit

Venus

You take my penis bravely, we're engineering 'we'
Since you creep in my thoughts, you're nearing me, you've never feared the 'we'

Inching into infinity...

You roll your touch around my neck as my tongue and your earlobe elope
You grope, I stroke, the glass ceiling of pleasure broke, the room smokes

You lip...

Grant me your breath and I'll make sure to hold it in highest regards
You've provided the chart; your constellation in my mind's sky is brilliantly large

I'm impregnated by your resilient posture; I'm gracious to see you exist
In my heart and also in this white, blue, and green ball that fits within God's fist

Grant me your voice; I'll make sure it enters the world's ears
I'll use it to redirect the peers who consider leaping from piers...

And... to cancel the courageous' fears

This is who I am, this is who you are
You're my finest hour, my guiding light, you are my star

I lip... Highness...

You encompass a science that I'm eyeing as the seconds are no longer flying
This lion is vying to be your jungle king and I'm not lying

You have to be defined as precious, most accurately, heavenly
The aged wine of your glance depicts the texture of your reverie

I have to have at least the better half of me...
To mesh with the best half of thee, it equals perfect math to me

You cause my pause, all I can do is parade my circus of cheer
The sheets between you and angels must be sheer and this is a divine mirror...

My eyes that is... and what I see in you is what I know resides in me

You are responsible for sailing my passion the highest, my highness
You possess the elements of a wife and that's why our chemistry is a science

And I tell you, Cupid's construction teams couldn't build better walls of loving

Feed me

I crave for the liquid that your body has made
The truest elixir available is able to raise love from the grave

It's heavy; it sits on my lips and slips onto my tongue
The mass of your watery class sinks into my mouth, to taste heaven is why my technique runs

Feed me

I want to taste the melanin within the skin of your bronzed golden tone
Why wouldn't I want to add hundreds of X's and O's and tic-tac-toe your X chromosomes?

With...

My legs are over yours; your legs are over mine
Our hair locks together, as we become intertwined into a vine

Time stood still with photographic memory, we moved invisibly
The room's four walls flattened and exposed mid-air sky walkers quite vividly

We were... living free... we were...

Beautiful, encompassing, warm, loving
Spicy, tingly, noteworthy, bubbling

Sunny, admirable, passionate, romantic
Anti-frantic, psycho somatic, tantric

Friendly, courteous, distinguished
Eternal, undiminishable, unfinished

It was...

Heavenly, angelic, hot, steamy
Fantastic, ethereal, intangible, dreamy

Innate, extroverted, royal, high
Regal, supreme, thoughtful, wise

Open, pure, priceless, authentic
Ancient, abysmal, unaugmented

Continuous, free, repetitive
Elite, exclusive, secretive

And because...

We've reigned before weather; This is to last forever
We've been greater before Good's pregnancy had bore Better

I want the world to know that your oatmeal palace rooms a womb of priceless value
I've written you into my life as my wife, the image of my pen pal is true

What we're making is...

The art of noise, the colors that we can't hear
It's the random structure of love, it's what Fear fears

It's a dream referred, it's the curve of words
It's the pressure of relief, the action linked to verbs

It's the vision of night; it's the mother to the sun
It's why the beginning had begun; it's a ladder without rungs

What we're making is...

The fairy's tails, the pixie dust, the fables
It's the comfort of steamy water when relaxation bathes you

It's female, male, man, thing
It's in between the seams of scenes in themes that can't be seen

It melts like snow and is incapable of hurting
It's name is pronounced by diamonds, it translates the birds chirping

It's solid, liquid, gas, it's white and black
Black and white, it's the spectrum of gamut whose location can't me mapped

What we're making is...

It's in all things yet outside of form
It's the sensation, the elation, the patience, it's not the norm

It's dark and dull while staying shiny and bright
It's the sounds of day and night, it's anti-fight

It's pro-fist, anti struggle, pro-pain, it's propane
It's a quiet explosion of logic that illuminates the slow shame

It's the faceless painting that's depicted in great detail
It's the reason Sally sells sea shells and the prism is in brain cells

It's captured and free, it's secluded openness
Its essence is wrote in this, it's mixed with hope and grit

And

Grime and time, reason and rhyme
It's questionably the answer to why we even have a mind

One story that tries describing us reads...

They became giants in the bedroom, he was her intergalactic groom
She swept across the cosmos as a model of perfection; the end was never coming
soon

They buzzed and weaved like threading honey bees
Deemed esteemed in dreams, a sowing this diligent proved they'd have more
sense than a full grown money tree

Hurricanes of typhoons weren't as wet as her fall when she was properly balanced
Exquisite flavor, artistic texture, her body applauded every time it managed his
talent

It's been told that...

His kisses would tip toe across her clit, they'd drop to catch every drip
Her mind tripped remembering their sunny summer day dazes when he navigated
the mazes of her hips

They spun worlds, danced until drenched in meteor showers
Spoke in places where time didn't exist, they did this for hours

He absolutely loved being lost within the waves of her sauce
He absolutely loved being tossed into the creamery of her frost

She loved him fishing for her tonsils as she threw him into her jaws
He loved enjoying the dreams but more of the reality of when he receive her all

They were gone from their physical lives so long that they've become dreams

Yet, we're currently creating another one

Since our dawns in the autumn air of Paradise, you've absorbed my orb
Your spiritual rituals are embedded in our mattress, I further erect to fill your
gorge

My body elates... your body shakes

Release unto my shaft the syrup of nature, I'll attest to Mrs. Butter's Worth
Allow it to leak and accumulate on my mid-section, my naval welcomes the surf

My Sexual Chocolate, consume my mind, let's leave this sack sapped
Until my honey nuts, your pleasure will be the breakfast that my heart attacks

You bite my lower lip and encourage me to go further without ever speaking a
word
My kisses become birds, pecking your neck, your cheek, your breast, the texture
of your body's curve

My thrusts in and out of your womanly seam seems to strengthen me
The way you seize my speed weakens your strong grip on my neck and the length
of me...

Dives to even greater depths...

50

I hear what's inside your mind...

You say...

You enter my creamy cave with precision
You turn your hips; twirl your dips, you pump like pistons in an engine

Forcefully... elliptically

Fast then slow, slow and then fast
I sail contentment in sighs that make me forget all earthly lovers from this pass

My breast become melded with yours, my body is yours
The passion starts to boil the flowing emotion, the water starts to steam and roar

You ease around me and spin my body into a cyclone
It's like a nice poem; you tongue my mind with kisses that I feel in my bones

Oh my...

You delve within the folds of my vaginal shelves
It's good as hell, my heaven, you keep dropping erect nickel into my wishing well

Orgasms begin to ripple deep in my ocean

I dissert our demonstration to the Galaxy's ears

It's like we dance throughout this dream, he leads the steps
I grab hold of his commitment, I've been wanting for this song since we've met

He glides me, he slides me, he's inside me
I escape into the throes of his soul as he pulls moons to entice my tide's sweep

And my tide sweeps toward "Us"... and...

We fall into the other
He uses the crimson gust of wind from our moves as our cover

His touch is teaching, I'm following his every lesson
A chiseled black angel and all mine, thank God for this blessing

Thank God

I don't know if I'm lying down, flying, or if I'm standing
My body is succumbing to the persistence of his loins; his reach is so demanding

I hug myself as his tongue sends shivers throughout my body
He palms my butt gently yet tightly, I feel that he's got me

Don't ever let me go

You dive into my neck and the emotions start surging
The room is becoming a river of passion and we're in its current

I dip my head back and throw my arms around his muscular back
He pulls me closer into his space, my heart attacks

Rubbing each inch of space that my walls offer...
His penis acts like it looks for his favorite orgasm of mine, looking to recover the lost purr

Our acapella moans are most harmonious on beds of music

Your persistent precision was predestined to progress into my perfect prescription

He wants me in a deeper sense, I feel him in my chest
Spasms flourish and I'm nourished within every atom of my flesh

You smile at my thoughts... allow me to continue with my descriptive declarative

My breasts fill my tongue's platter as your mouth feeds on my pleasure
Placing my arms and legs around you allows me to accept the entire heir of this orgasmic weather

You blow me away...

With your depth, strong gusts of passion sail me away

You blow me away...

You understand the atmospheric pressure between us and with angelic movements...

You blow me away... How ironic...

You studied astrophysics and psychology; you deposit tornados of love letters to my memory banks

He places me on his lap and we blossom into another dimension of love

Soft as petals we kiss seductive kisses; this is as pure as love
Eight inches of his four letters stuff into my envelope

I feel his entire stroke
The base of my spine vibrates and bolts

You blow me away...

With high deft defying acts of balancing sentiment and aggression, you never lose me

Your love blows me away...

You know of Karmic law and orbital charts, you know I'll be back if you blow me away

And as we lay, making love, I'm watching myself get blown away

Each time I bounce, each time that I further pounce
My grip accepts his strike and I slowly lose count

1,000, 2,000, 3,000 ... How many times have I come to this climax in our lives

I feel like an animal, we're breaking all the laws of 'love making'
It's supposed to be soft and gentle right, that old definition is getting replaced and...

Torn from the pages scribed by the ancient sages
God has blessed him in places that could turn an angel out of the faithless

He grinds and plows through my field of delight
He's given eternal entry, he's tilling the land, and he farms with such might

Yet with such accuracy, he pushes screams from me every time he pulls me close
My angel makes me see pure light; his divine diving is appreciated the most...

By my vagina

He mines my gold like a 49[er]
He's deep enough within my ocean to land within my inner China

He pulls me up and kisses whispers to the softest part of my brain
He's been my flame; he's burned his tattoo within the blood of my veins

He says through his touch he knew I always needed him
He's played inside of my gem like we were in gym; he's crème de le crème

My water falls like Niagara, it pools into the Milky Way

The Galaxy enjoys this tale... I give all to you... my man, speak

The testosterone in me is gracious as I continue to...

Fall into your abyss with tenderness, I inhale your scented gift
The mist of our elevating aroma that spins around the room causes my hands to lift

I raise your hips; passion raises the intensity of our kissing lips
Your arching back raises the depth of my adept dips

I can smell your achieved climax and I...

Retreat to savor the taste of your sours, salts, and sweets
I mouth your velvety richness; I inhale your syrup until I can't breathe

LOOK AT ME!!!

See me nibble your labias like quesadillas, the trembles make it hard to resist...

Screaming... gasping for air... searching for strength to speak

This is just the tip of the iceberg, just a paraphrasing gist of what tonight has in store for you... and

I continue to lip secrets as you further secrete

And

If your depth was debt and my tongue were legs, metaphorically I'd be knee deep

I've gotten a mouth full of your blackberry pie
This multiple orgasmic feeling is rushing through your body and painting tears to your eyes

While you're shaking and bucking your hips
My hands firmly hold your waist while my tongue still circles your clit

Tonight...

I'm truly acting as a carnivore, eating you and pleasing you more than you bargained for
With my arms fastened around your body, my passion acts with harnessed force

I turn and lift you over me

The penetration of my length gently kisses the tip of your cervix
My mission is to have you orgasm until your brain's memory merges...

This time of excellence with every past marvel that Love's ever made pass out of us

This friction, this unnameable flame we're constructing is growing hands
It's pulling us deeper in love, the depths of enlightenment sees our silhouetted stance

I provide my love as...

Gently yet as ferociously as the king of the jungle

You ride me as...

Passionately as Valentine's 14th plane yet as slowly and deliberately as Venus' yacht

I provide my love as...

Callisthenic as possible, stretching your lounge with deepening reps when I lunge through

You ride me as...

A radiantly charged Goddess since you're a panel atop this son's strongest solar prop

Heat indexes of Hell's previous forecasts can't equal our blaze
Picture perfect pixels of Paradise positioned in platinum portraits can't equal our daze

Interior decorators couldn't reposition her décor better
Swimming lessons with Poseidon submerged in the Atlantic with little mermaids couldn't get her wetter

You become vocal... airing expressions of fulfillment... I know that you've...

Realized my real eyes and my real vibe
Before there were gravity and real skies, our fate was already sealed tight

I know... and above all else...

Towards me, you'll always and genuinely express your love
It'll stay explicit and untainted until I lie in the hole that's dug

We both share an invisible conclusion that...

Come midnight, the heavens will have called us to action
Our silken fabric of ardency would have started unwrapping

You moan to me through bated breath... "Baby,"

The sweet utter of my name from your mouth freezes me
Your soft smile and see through stare deliberately tease me

Slight nibbles to my wrists collapse the running track of my mind
Even curious moon rays lean in and slip pass the half shut vertical blinds

I love you

I honestly love you, and I mean that I really love you
The way we spread across these sheets could be called poetry but I know the truth

We make love

Beautiful, fully exposed, bare it all love

We make a...

Blimp-like, monumental, earth rebirthing, never claimed to be small love

I know your every atom of my feminine feels the strength of my masculine

I savor your flavor and determine that you're in my favor
I read your articles of clothing; you're my current news event, now that's major

You've renewed what I've been dying to create
You've resurrected the spirit of Soul because before calendars we've had a date

We've had an absolute passion... and you search...

You expound on what's found, you echo my every sound
Your mystical liquid fills my lungs but I have never drowned

Never and you...

Magnify the exhaustion of my sighs, the vision of my eyes
You continuously provide the height for my high, the pulse keeping me alive

When I say that I love you, I know that you already know
Your fashion is always ready to show and you've been the formula to help this child grow

You don't necessarily have a coke bottle shape body but you got that pep, see
You unlock and let me, freely you direct me, and you sincerely respect me

You are my words

I love you; I love your every syllable
You make my desires lyrical, your pen is my raft and I'll keep floating on your miracle

And tenderly, we hold a glance, the passion in our eyes is simmering...

Our sweaty, bare, and embracing bodies love the touch
Moans of pleasure echo through the silences of the hush

Uhn... aaah... ahhh...

Guide my touch until your body showers blushes
Feel the width of my paddle stirring your waters, feel the rushes...

Rage through your skeleton

You've gotten karma sutra beat with your seemingly endless techniques
Bed sheets envelope our bodies while we let their rustlings interpret our speech

Feel the rushes rage through your spirit

The sweet warm winds of your nature surround my entity
My sensitivity increasingly grows from within me

Feel the rushes within strokes as I continue to sail it in

My nostrils fill with your smell, your mind fills with me
You've made yourself my personal blanket, you supply the heat

Feel the rushes continue to drip your soul in your tearing

Have you ever cried because you're being pleased that nicely
I lean you close to kiss your sugar lips, you pour out more samples of your iced
tea

Your body answers... Yes! Yes!! Yes!!!

And know that before I met you...

I still dreamed of you
Still felt the steam from the passionate flare that esteems from you

Still...

Cared for you
Still was conscious of the fact that my lungs fill with the air of you

Still

Watched the slide show slide slow as my eye lids glide low
Unrolled and strolled scrolls of the beautiful bridges of our love's toll

Know that...

I still write about you

And

Arranged the solutions for all the things that aren't right about you

My solutions drew the face of you

I've always seen you and freed you from my mouth with the sentences when I'd
speak of you
My heart still leaked of you and even today my perfumed lips still reek of you

And...

I still think of you in the still of the night
Let's continue to steal the night, and continue to feel the son steel the light

You remain in my thoughts... you state...

My King...

You traverse within my inner Earth; you're ensuring our future's birth
Of what do you search, my climaxes come in waves and you're the first to surf

We'll once again make time halt... Honey...

My passion is blazing for you; you've been the imagery of poetic phrasing
You impregnate me with patience, you are so, so amazing

I lean into you... our foreheads are touching... I gently speak

"I need more of you and for every grain of sand on the sea shores
I'll give reason for why I adore you, to why I need more...

Of... you

You've steered clear to my pleasure and have never dismissed our intimate moments

I always knew we were on the same page even though I spoke in words while you spoke in symbols
Life has grown simple, our emotions clash like passionate cymbals, and we no longer try, we are gentle

And... as if I had slipped from a pier...

I've drowned myself with you in my thoughts as I stayed around my peers
Never forget that I still possess that sinking feeling for you, right here...

In the pit of my stomach... Every day, I fall back in love with you"

You acknowledge my genuine confession...

You respond...

"I want to be your best friend, your first, your last, your only
The one who always comes with action when you ask can you show me

I want to make you feel special and I don't ever want to let you...
Step through, any pain alone and with my all, I promise to protect you"

I repeat... "With my all... I promise to protect you"

I'm the last one to see you leak, the first granting what your soul seeks
You're the one for me; you get me hot to degrees that make me freeze

You listen as I further articulate more of my thoughts into words...

"For the rest of life, we'll be husband and wife
You've stolen my heart, my mind and soul within one night

You've organized the perfect heist... For the duration of this night... I intend to thoroughly please you"

Know that I am...

The swirl of calligraphy, passion plus infinity
I am the unmistakable shock of reality, I'm creative energy

I am a scientist, I'm why eyes exist
I've been the 'why' in this receiving the largest share; I have a lion's wish

Your eyes cry a reply

I'm your woman

I sit beside thee, we stand in planets, our knees are sky deep
No woman's love matches my flame, I'm the source supplying the heat

Speaking of myself in the third eyes of third persons

You, son, burn for her, Eternity yearns for her
Wisdom learned from her, and every direction to freedom turns to her

I'm your better half, the whole and sole reason for breathing
Your soul's reason for being, I am your heart, the only fairy tale you believe in

I'm inspiration, I'm dedication, and I am the ending
I'm your angel presented in perfect angles, I'm in all women

We're as inseparable as the seas and shores, perspective and views
You're as dynamic as the purest prism that has collected the hues

Because not only do you reflect every color of love...

You reflect every color of me
My soul's gradient is forever radiant; I'm the complimentary color of he

Which is you... my dream man

You collect the message my eyes telegraph and add to it

As a kid I wished for you... I...

Couldn't wait for your body to be the embodiment of my poetic sentiment
You'd have captured Heaven within your scent and expel the highest intelligence

If we shall be absolutely perfect for only such a brief moment...

Let that moment be now and...

Let the keys to Eternal Love live in your series of blissful moaning

I always knew you'd be more than beautiful... more than lovely

Your personality would flow like my rhyme scheme
You'll steam throughout my arteries using my veins as vines to swing

Since I became aware of my imagination...

I saw the day your rich kisses would be deposited into my memory banks

And when...

The mattress holds your coming attraction you wouldn't be an actress, and I'll
tenderly thank...

Every inch of mahogany magnificence with lips full of appreciation
You're indelible, you're the ink of what I think that can't be erased and...

Forgotten... and for years...

I've written about you while sitting daydreaming about your grace
Your face and waist, your taste and the love we'd make

On many occasions

I've drifted off into the ecstasy knowing that I'll one day share whatever is left of
me
I've been sea sick from the vicissitudes of love, but I still yearn for such a love
quite respectively

I simply couldn't wait for our connection; I knew it'd be divine
For your graphic is the only reason that my imagination was designed

And now it's happening... we're making reality from my dreams

So I'll moan and groan for you since basically I've grown for you
Our one fabric is too delicate to rip now since we've been sewn from two

What if I told you that everything I've shown you...

Was magnetically charged to hold you
I've never tried to own you but renting space in your mind's place makes it my
home too

Feel me... so...

Get used to the groove
Every motion you move mimics the rhythm of jewels, I'm visually drawn to you

The italicized words I speak lean into your imagination and soak into your brain
tissue
This is my main issue, am I not a terrorist if I send your mental plane missiles

Aren't I'm not

I only aim to break down and destroy woman's nonchalant façade
The vapors of our heat creates a legitimate visage, this is not a mirage

My description is of a man and that'll be what I am to you... always... and of my love...

You can grab this and wrap this within the folds of your eyelids
Find it as a kind kit that supplies our hiking hearts the reason to keep on climbing

Speak of me as your most sought after dream, let me roll off of your tongue
Remain in this childlike innocence; fraternize through the map of skies with the
son of Suns

And I'll...

Continue to position you in open seclusion, populated isolation
Only when my vision is fading have we mated, and only when we've seen it, have
we made it

You are my diamond... Diamond...

I know that the strength of a woman is what you embody
The hues of your glittering, attractive, reflection translates the language of Beauty's
hobby

Tell me why you shine, why you can capture everyone's attention
The mystique you leak through visual doors relieves the mystery of soulful tension

One can't be angry while concentrating on your features
A girl's best friend may well indeed prove to be a man's most valuable teacher

For your elusive height of perfection, adventurous eyes will keep climbing
Stay abundant with your affectionate glare; I'll always take care of you, Diamond

Your soul peers into my own as your waist steers upon my erect throne

I hold you as you are holding me
Skating on my rail while my hips wave like rolling seas have you soaking, please...

Let your body perceive my intuition, let this experience be extra sensory

I want your soul, your mind, your wishes and concerns
You have the lesson I want to learn and the only curves I want to turn

Over and over and over again

You guide my touch in such a sexy way that the blinds show a blush
Our room's atmosphere feels the width of my paddle stirring your waters into a rush

Even now, it's getting warmer

We've built an attraction with the memories we've placed on mental shelves

That...

When we peek inside the other's mind we realize that we're looking at ourselves

I see your eyes rolling back to a previous session of love making

You reminisce the imagery of one of our lives...

I...

Cover your screams with kisses while I grab your attention

You...

Teeth my chest and neck as you come to find that this archer never misses his mark

I...

Keep reaching and inching and inching and reaching upwards towards your inner dimensions

You...

Etch hieroglyphics on my back; you leave my flesh marked

We both love it

Your angelic wings of love ground me while you're surrounding me
You're astounding me with the movements of your body while we're lounging free

Precipitating and sprinkling passion into our erotic oil
We wrap our attraction into a coil until our sweat boils

I remember one year, years and years ago, in a California hotel...

We wrestled chocolate desires in a Westin's west end suite
You'd peek sweeps of heaven when you'd slide and glide your honeyed physique

You moaned moons of tunes as planets spun themselves out of space
We collided vibes and, with tides and, we drew passion from the other though we had no face

We only had energy

You embroidered soul with your finger nails while threading the seams of my heart with your name
You held lungs of fire, windpipes full of gasoline and uttered pleasure with flames

We challenged our shadows to see whose love making would outlast the other
We ignored insecurities; inhibitions were missing but witnessed the birth of Nature's mother

We orchestrated the authentication of existence; you knew we'd eventually relapse
Our ebbing orgasms never attempted to retract; bottled light had the night capped

Our sexual pressure vied to have it pop... yet I remember

65

We wrestled chocolate desires in a Westin's west end suite

And

You slumbered for an eternity awake in my dreams as I am the memory of us
when you're asleep

So, Sweetheart, don't you remember being my Muse?

While you still sit on me... The dripping moisture of your lake confirms...

You retell the account

It would come mid-night on most nights that I was called to action
Our silken fabric of ardency started unwrapping, your mind is entrapped and...

Entertained by this ghostly flame that heated up your main frame
I'm such a strange dame; my kisses are as sweet as raw sugar cane

I slowly pulled out your pen, its ink was already leaking from the tip
I rubbed around the circumference with my mouth and then sat on it

Dress rehearsal was over...

You were engaged in the bright scene of a ménage a twilight
My movements, reminiscent of marijuana smoke. caught you in my high life's
highlight

In pleasure's bright light...

You breathed heavier; my tongue was an acrobat within your mouth
You spoke my passion; this is what channeling is all about

You were, amazing... you spiced up the night like you were Cajun

Your touch was stuck on my hips, I opened my lips
You scream, "Baby, please, please keep stroking it"

I'm your Muse, baby... You're obliged

I took your talent to the summit's peak and then made it rise
Your eyes became my eyes, my essentials and your essence would collid, you felt more alive

I've created this world for your creative mind... you're the King of the Palace of Mastery

Here...

Dead batteries of crafted speech are recharged rapidly

Here...

Calamities have to be received happily, you have to marry seas

You have to...

Swim in gyms of gems, where sins are whims
Where lights can't dim, heroes are every him, where love grows from every limb's stem

I've created this world for your creative mind to rule... and together...

We over flow every rim and cup every constellation at its cusp
There are no I's, breathing lungs can only We's and everyone is us

We only mourn written poems of valiant ink; they're the only ones dying
Every iris is Irish; every cherished treasure chest belongs to the pirates...

Of caring beings

The smooth mires of desire help give cadence to the angels high up...
Whose voices blaze throughout the skies like mass choirs of fire and I'm no lyre

But...

I'm strung from being stung and I won't stop spinning comprehension...
Until mental eyes choose not to glisten and hearts to passionate chivalry choose not to listen

I, a woman... God in feminine flesh... and

I'll keep spinning straw into gold because I've been told to unspool my soul
I'm too cool to be cold, I can't own these odes so I present them to you, keep them close

Yet know that...

Being separated cannot keep me away from you
I'm within every element that creates you; we'll always find a way to renew

I'm the one that gave your imagination boundless potential

Understand that my absence is what makes this connection strongest

And I'm here to ensure that...

Bad times can't manipulate the Writer's writings of rites to ever become the wrongest

And here, back in your room, on this plane of Present's mind

Your spirit is blessing me, we fall into an ecstasy
We paint the walls next to me with shadows of love as artistically as sexually

I'm taking in the entire heir, what's left to breathe... I roll off and over to expose my lunar sea

With my elbows attached to my knees and my face being one with the mattress
You've perfected your practice; I know my bouncing bumper is being waxed with...

Slow strokes that are incredibly stiff, this is an uneditable clip

You grip my hips to further push into my abysmal pond
I float within the laughs of your spiritual gloat; of this feeling, I'm too fond

Your vine's divine ability to climb up spines to cerebral cortexes is sublime

I gently return the thrust; I rock against your stone

I raise my hips; passion raises the intensity of our kissing spirits
My arching back raises the depth of your twisting dips

55 lives ago, 1,000 years ago, 500,000 moons ago

I fast forward to previous sounds of this sexual odyssey
You're taking all that I have to give without ever even robbing me

From the huts of Native American belief...

You've been the catcher of my dreams

From the igloos of Alaska...

You've frozen me with romantic hands

From the chambers of Our Pyramids...

You pampered me with regality, my king

From the androgyny of asexual galaxies...

It's been easily decipherable, you are definitely all man

I reach back to you and you clasp hands with me

This connection was felt when we drafted The Plans
Crafted the lands, tanned the sands, and left the breeze in front of the fan

I reach back to you and you clasp hands with me... it was...

Wild hair, wow stares, wild's fair...
When used to describe what we did while there...

While here... Making love being infinite signs at Studio 54

Laying in the middle of our sexual mayhem
Say damn, the feelings I feel are supreme, I wouldn't dare say grand

You scream, I scream
We both scream while licking off and swallowing all cream

You played out fantasy roles I've only dreamt of

While...

My playboy model body got unfolded and pinned up

We've sent up...

Enough love sighs that cupid covered his eyes

And

Wild's fair, when talking about what we did when we covered the night

Your hands taste the flavor of my spine as I further obligate myself to bind with thy vine
Exercising private muscles rings our cerebellums until the time for orgasms chime

11:11pm

You're deep in my court yard of passion

You're swaying my structure of love

Your powerfully deep strokes take me to the edge and nudge

I'm falling into a realization of cause and effect and this is how we've happened

It's because we've made Love that in turn, Love made us

The silver lined arms of the moon fondle the blinds for a peek
They ease around the defense as thunder rumbles after a flash of lightning streaks

Baby...

I give the baton of pleasure to you and place my hands within the bed's sheets
You reach to my navel as I bathe you, you decode the message my body speaks

Take over my existence King, man, let your sexual prowess wow this, woman

Indeed my love... Know that...

Your heat filled moans and tones and the warmth of your hold...
Makes me feel like I'm taking a shower on the sun as I hydroplane on this sexually wet road

With the sheets wet like sea diving, you, again, are arriving
With yells colliding, around, pleasure pours from your vocal rising, your soul's
reviving

And until...

The sea of sheets are wrecked, until this mattress is off set

And until...

You've gotten all you can get, I know that seconds for dessert is all set

So...

Every minute I'm witness to this event, hours of our past relives
Paris, Egypt, Japan, we've left every space we've faced love filled

You're the wealth of Woman, even without bars of gold or coins of silver...
It's your benevolence that tills dirt until hurt dissolves leaving only love to fill
Earth

We've...

Frolicked through the fields of fornication

We've

Connected on a molecular level, we've engaged in more than mating

Remember...

We're rocked stars, seen mountains of settled angel dust
Flashed light years through circular perspectives, our range robust

If our love could ever be read wrong...

Label me illiterate

If our passion no longer thumps...

Label me a bass drum with a little kick

If our love is no longer patient...

Label me bed written, I'll only be a little sick

And if our love ever looks wrong...

Label my ignorance naïve because I'll refuse to see it

Your sweat permeates with the certainty of Allure's scent
The invisible rivers of Seduction have sprayed you with mists of allurement

And as...

Night's hands shadow one half of your flesh
My hands cover the rest; my touch becomes a coat of caress

You body is soft to my touch

Your body...

Is too loving for lust

Your body...

Is so soft to my lips

Your body...

Is too loving to forget

I can't spend any life without you... I will always find you

You're my soul's most sincere desire

You've been and will always be what I know as truth
I've been and will always be yours and I won't ever have to re-mine you

You are some kind of wonder

And within the World of the Wondrous... you're as beautiful as...

Hazel eyes with an Aruba sunset colored pupil

You're as beautiful as...

Distant dreams spoken through the adjectives of a romantic painter's rose colored brush

You're as beautiful as...

Visions of Heaven's fashion show on Imagination's stage in Paradise

You're as beautiful as...

Seeing diamond rain drops fall to reveal a golden rainbow

And as my lips fall to your fountain

I extract the juices of your ageless and unbound confectionery
I admit our affinity in ancient tongue and though the languages of confessions vary...

You totally understand and comprehend

Pleasurably severe wonder storms through our nerves and mind
Cataclysmic orgasms are being created, worlds of passion swirl and swerve in lines

From the World of the Wondrous to the galaxies of fantasies...

Passion reeks from our majesty as we assembled their structures quite lavishly
Our love has spoken in each and every crafted suite though our voices have never had to speak

Feel me... re-enter...

I'll love you as long as...

An ever expanding, infinitely enduring eternity

I'll love you as long as it takes...

Falling chameleons to convince Autumn that they're showing their true colors

I'll love you as long as it takes...

The repeating reoccurrence of Reminisce's rendezvous to stop its stutter

I'll love you as long as...

The echo of wishes and if's is, until viewers of Existence's closing curtain deceases

I'll love you for forever... and a day

And now, currently in this bed

I slowly withdrawal from your creamy cove, you spin around and then crawl to me
What you send to me is a pleasure that only a pure connection could lend to me

Your mouth and hands are working congruently in moving me
Your maneuvering of insane acuity exchanges my rationale from logic to lunacy

This is crazy

You look up to me, I look up to you
I can hear the rolling thunder in the distance as the rain pitter patters the roof

I push you back and slide you to the edge of the bed and now I kneel before you
I position your hips downward so that your vaginal carafe allows me to pour you

I've always pondered...

Which set of your lips tasted the best
You permit me to soul search, for my tongue to sink within your absorbent flesh

Of our kisses and of our positions

We share a sexually voracious appetite

This hunger is

Insatiable, irreplaceable, it's golden delicious, it's apple like

My exploring tongue finds itself surveying a shaved savanna that's multi-tiered

And...

Your traveling residue of satisfaction finds itself settling on my beard

While growing into my greatness, I've felt you

I'm drawn by your soul and outlined by the glittering shade of you
It's true; I'm honest and modest yet far from a novice when I do what I do

I knew I'd capture my dream

You've been captivated by my forceful gentleness
I've sent you kiss, after kiss through line of poems that emit your sense

I've written volumes about your vanity, trilogies about being your eternal lover

You've become my metaphorical lotion after my proverbial showers of struggle
You're my supplemental mentor and trainer, you've help me sculpt new and desirable muscle

Know that I love you

You, the all knowing, and ever present you
I live with you in my soul so when people look into my eyes they'll see Heaven shine through

Feel it... I immensely enjoy pleasing you

My tongue laps a criss cross over your clit soft until I wear your lips' gloss
The sheets are ripped off, no drips lost; they're caught until 900 seconds tick off

Within the first 100 seconds...

100 blessings are delivered as shivers as hot as a flaming winter

Tick...

Throughout 200 seconds...

Your soul feels 200 sensations racing, raising the hair of your fleshed casing

Tick... Tick...

Licking for 300 seconds...

While I roam erotic zones, you moan and groan, body boiling, the tea pot's whistles been blown

Tick... Tick... Tick...

The final 300 seconds...

Prove orgasmic, gigantic, galactic attacks hit, I manage to view Heaven's hue at a tongue's point of vantage

You let out a bellowing howl of delight that reawakens the primal desires I share for pleasing you

I recall...

Open grasslands where our legs and hands danced

Where...

The eyes of Romance glance, seeing the movements from our slow pant's chant

I recall...

Your feminine dividends did a bend with ligament of elastic cinnamon

Where...

Tender meant to simmer sense into a flaming sea to coast our un-censorship

We were so delicate yet we forgot how not to be rough

It was raw, it is raw
It's all we saw, it's what we always taught

I'd bite at your neck; you'd grab and squeeze my loins
We'll never stop going, we seamed perfectly as the hands of Fate kept its thread sewing

In ancient times...

We coiled into erotic symbols, erotic shapes, and erotic meaning
We're immortalized in forgotten script, scribed in the visual vibes of dreams and...

That invisible force that attracts two people together

I arise from my knees to reinsert myself in the center of your life

Oh... my... Goddess...

I'm embossed in the rising waters of your glossy ocean's beveling sea
The feeling of pure pleasure itself pales in comparison to the delight of your delicacies

The concentrated cream I receive from my concentrated means lines my penis like a pin-stripe suit

Your cream...

Streaks down upon my thick shaft as slowly as Molasses descending in zero gravity with a parachute

Your cream...

Crawls down my erection enjoying every inch of the brown plains it migrates across

Your cream...

On top my sleek, steep slope, secretes retreats of sweet heat until your rolling eyes get lost

But yet... you follow me... because...

Your clutch is as tight as it was before
Of my love, by the attention I keep persistent, you'll be sure

Through my visions of recollecting our ever present image of love... you speak to me

Baby, I'm falling into the height of a high that's as deep as...

A universe that's as tall as the width of ten galaxies

Your love penetrates and delves into me as deep as...

Abysmal rivers of wisdom streaming into boundless oceans of thought

Your love penetrates and delves into me as deep as...

The roots of the tree of life within the ground of God's imagination

I'm falling into the height of a high that's as deep as...

Bass chanting monks meditating in subterranean chambers of fascination

I welcome your greeting of depth as...

Your penis peaks, peeks, sneaks, creeps, I leak from deep, I reap since you sought

You reach with a thirst for questing as deep as...

The writings of a profound poet buried in the submerged floor of bottomless ceilings which floats upward through negative gravity

You stroke deeply...

Like painters in submarines asleep dreaming of being underground drawing pictures of the abyss

You stroke deeply...

I encompass your every direction as you map new worlds of climax to my cervix

Your words shall always prove to me that you're forever my prints charming

New ideas of making love run through my mind with the endurance of time
The way your thrust is rocking my body, my breasts are jumping as if I'm on Pegasus flying

I soar through stimulated atmospheres emulating what they see happen here
Thunderous waves pound and an electric flash appears...

I know that if Love is blind and Passion is deaf...

Even eyeless...

I'd still see the aura of your blazing magnificence

And... even earless...

I'd still hear the genuineness of your persistent lisp

You're the archetype designed by The Architect to never become parched from
sex
Our connection is eternal and it'll stay that way even after our spirits and souls
part from flesh

We're figures of the art of Intimacy; we share a stare, intimately
I'm deepening in you while feeling the depth of your devotion entering me

And then... STOP... everything stops... time... sound... our movement

Silence drowns the room, it's quiet enough to hear nothing
Rain drops fall in pane as we lay motionless; we begin to float into nothing

My hair raises from our pillow and flies into your face
The covers that blanketed us release their weight; they fall into the ceiling that
serves as a grounded base

I float back above you...

I state through the cortex

You pull my hair and it's as if you remove my earthly mask
Every second yet spent accumulates into a now that I will always have

I can start to see through you, you're literally becoming transparent

Your hands grasp mine, our lips clasp into a kiss
We dematerialize and disappear, leaving the room in a whimsical whiff

Whew

We're on the verge of entering an unfathomed millennium's ear
Our love will be heard, and the realization of our soul will be clear

As clear as...

The articulated point of transparent diamonds

As clear as...

The obvious reasons why aspiring conquerors keep on climbing

It's to achieve oneness... and that's what we're doing... we seem to be...

Surrounded within a labyrinth of rose bushes overlooked by towering oaks
Tears of crystal run to my ears as you swing overpowering strokes

The greenest grass tickles my neck and conforms to the weight of perfection
You mouth kisses to my soul's windows and feel the mist of my jubilant expression

I've only ever truly allowed you to let me down... I've only allowed you the treasures within my mound

You yell through the grip of your hands, I speak through my watery eyes
I had Love's song memorized; eventually I knew a time would come for you to witness her daughter's reprise

I'll sing for you, baby... anytime you want me to

The skies eye psychics to see the true power of Midas
Every eternal lover once touched by their soul mate infects them with the wellness of Infinititis

The only sickness that heals the hurt of reality... the only sickness to bring eternal happiness

Eagles and hawks squawk loudly into the air, we can hear their soaring speech
I hold your face while I kiss your cheeks and please you aurally

I state in seductive, airy breath

"Baby, this soil is for your planting, your kisses, your seeds, your staff
Wind up your wind of wood and every tornado of rough drafts you craft I'll provide the aquatic rocking for you to raft

I'll take all of your mighty pleasure, baby… this loving is indestructible"

Birds of every color fly to finally see the grounded sky walkers
Our entire existence is based on the preservation of Love and to keep it fostered

Every eye blink is like the shutter of a time traveling camera…

You're captured

Our memories share your masculine scent

I'm kissing your collar bone as we lay across jet black sands

I picture…

A gentle breeze of silk-like kisses sweeping and massaging you without my hands

Picture this

Lying naked in a hammock with my breasts filling your mouth

And I remember the picture…

Using the fabric of my dress to muffle my screams and to muffle my shouts…

As you went down on me while the elevator was going up

But, as we're surrounded by everything yet nothing… I feel you

You please me intentionally, you move in me with a purpose
You labor onto me a love that ensures and guarantees that our love maker keeps working

I question you and boast to you through my rhythm

You love this don't you? Will you allow me to pour out my love over you for forever… or until I run dry?

You nod to answer but can tell by my smirk that I know I'll always rain my sexual reign over you

You look deeply in my eyes as I ride, as I drop and as I rise
No crash as we collide, gentle, nimble slides provide sight to a new set of ahhh's

*For the ones that can envision this kind of pleasure... we move as
delicately as an angel being born mid-air into their wings*

I can feel you pulse inside of me; this is the action that brought life to be
I hold your chest, you hold my breast, I hold my breath while my expressions vie
to breathe

Slow movements in a cyclic motion only accentuate my devotion
I encourage you; my wine whines for you, fill me with your erotic potion

Please... baby... please

My job as your eternal lover is to satisfy your every desire, your every yearn
To take your unformed thoughts of clayed resemblance and shape them into
something firm

Something that's...

Tangible, memorable, wonderful and breathtaking

Something that's...

Timeless, magical, the product created within Eternity's making

And...

We continue to fall through Space like we've fallen off the edge of a flat world

And

Glints of light hint that this is just a stint of time while our passion howls
throughout this black swirl

There will be light again... yet, within this silence...

We continue to fall through Space like...

The flakes of a snow globe in slow rolls upon the imperceptible waves of our
soul's hold

And...

We decided in glides in spiraling strides of remembered honey combed lives to always confide in this pose...

With each other and... I hear your manly mentions admit...

The taste of your body delights my tongue and elates my hands
Your flesh feels my touch run as wildly as crazy herds of untamed beasts over thigh'd lands

Tonight, there are no rules... we will be...

Lawless, flawless

Let's vow to never awe less than the sight of the full spread wings of angels made of a pure solitaire diamond's zest

Succulent, delectable, mouth-watering and luscious
I can't get enough, miss, my breath is coated with the flavor of your heavenly muffin

My beard is showered by the unlimited springs of your essence
Your moans fill the air of four walls while your clitoris hears my tongue whisper an eternal message

With an energy to hinder speech, render your shriek, yet only allows your whimpers to leap, yet only allows your whimpers to leap
I'll always be here to keep you coming an orgasm that'll surge pleasure from the depths of your inner sea

Attentive pleasure and tireless devotion casts an unbreakable bond
I ease up and bend your legs back to fully allow my love to expound

Your eyes lean into my sight... your stare states... my man, husband to be... my wish is that...

You continue to strum my vaginal harp with fingers full of skill, a tongue full of technique

My wish is that...

You continue to give me plump kisses from full lips and deliver your deep, strong strokes that keeps me weak

You continue to listen as feminine energy envelops our bodies

Until my eyes are as red as the rivers of lost love and I can escape night
I'll keep my sadomasochistic sentence submissive to my Muse's strike

You're the one that inspires me

My passion was crafted with the same pencil you sharpened for my architectural drafting
I've sailed minds with lyrical mines to wave the thoughts of our brains but never rushed waters for rafting

Our saga has...

Freed hearts from rib cages, our love's style will forever trend in fads of poetic phrases

And...

For the silhouettes of ghosts who are scared to face their own shadowed faces, I'll grant them patience

Know that...

I'll remain self-ish and vein only a pure blood of reign
My eyes reside in a passionate flame; I'm the only heir your lungs can truly claim

I'm egotistically humble; I'll mute the whispers when my hatred mumbles

And

I'll always be the spirit to serve nutritious food for thought when empty imaginations start to grumble

So understand, baby... When our mental desires take shape, we open a gateway

Us making love is more than just you having your penis inside of me
It's more than spending romantic time with me, more than me serving you the
finest feast

It's more than that... it's more than...

Flesh gripping, nail digging, hopping hips, hard dropping dips

It's more than that... it's more than...

Glazed lips, rolling eye flips, orgasmic trips or having reality and fantasy mix

*When our mental desires take shape, we open a gateway... and it's
about...*

Your arousal starting before I unbuckle your trousers

It's about...

Seduction allowing the bow of my present's arch to encourage you to have its and
yours smile merge

It's about how you...

Consume the flavor of Love, taste the warmth of the tea once the kettle is turned
on
Tongue the lyrics of Yearn's song, I provide the music and best sheets to learn on

This is more than sex... we make love

From having my locked ankles draped across your neck

To...

Having your locked eyes on mine as you watch my mouth flex

We make love

From my face's grimace as I feel you penetrate pass my limits when you're in it

To...

Riding erupting surfs to shores of Sure when you ask if I love how you tend and bend it

WE MAKE LOVE... and...

I curl to you, I sway with you, forever shall I stay with you
I'll gray with you; there isn't an element nor promise that I'd trade for you

And baby, know that...

Whoever's touch has briefly held you before I came into this life to reclaim you...

I promise that they'll never feel you again

Whoever's voice turned your head before I came into this life to reclaim you...

I promise that their call will never reach you again

Whoever's loving you had before I came into this life to reclaim you...

I promise that you'll never long for that again

Whoever left you and did you wrong before I came into this life to reclaim you...

I promise that the sight of you and I will remind them again and again

I am the one that they could never be... you were the one that they could never really have... You are mine

What's a fling compared to the force that's making the universe swing
This is the table that I set, what more could any woman bring

I question, man... I answer all... They could never compare to me

Someone please build mountain high steps so...

They'll see that with my vision, they could never stare with me
I have split personalities of excellence and perfection, no other tandem of
personas could ever come pair with me

*I state... I am the answer... I'm the woman that comes paired with
thee*

What I see in you is why I always find reasons to keep coming back

When I was a small girl, I wrote letters to the wind hoping they didn't blow off my
wishes
I prayed to the Heavens for Cupid to find a marksman with impeccable aim, I
prayed not for his misses...

*But to be his misses... and when I was a small girl... for as long as I
can remember...*

I've been obsessing over how tender your gender would be in removing my soul's
winter
Now, with you deep inside of me, my spirit burns with the heat of the sun at its
most essential center

While I penned in my diary...

I was in another world when I was writing; we created a world that was so exciting
A collage of colliding kaleidoscopic canvases covered what I was eyeing, what I
was describing

I arranged mystical miracles from the midst of myths
I was an author creating the physical equivalent of if's, I caused Love's paradigm
to shift

I became an intergalactic Ruler of Imagination as we doctored Destiny's patience
I simultaneously wrote present and past tense so no matter which way Janus was
facing...

They saw life breathe... they see the pictures that my ink bleeds

This is my mind exposed; this is what the universal whispers have always told
How could I have known my pen of mines explodes and enlivens so many dying
souls, this path of love is our chosen road

This world of mind is spectacular, you, my sun, are an amazing raisin
I wrote about the periphery of the adjacent, about the height that the mirage is raising

Our work on this planet is subject to objectivity, the object of subjectivity
Erase my words and we would still live, our spilling images have stained brains, there's no getting rid of me...

Or you

Currently, with your every passion flushed glance and the reminiscence of our before life stance...

For as long as I've thought, you've been what I've sought; I know that my man is worth his salt

And each lesson taught...

Deepens our love, surrounding me with the notion that once again within the vault of love, I'm caught

I'm caught... Your mind interjects...

Baby, I feel you baby... and I recognize that...

You have wrecking eyes that break down my calm reserve and encouraged the lesser guy in me to step aside
Leaving my reason to become your destined guy justified, what we experience is the best of lives

In whatever life, during whatever time

Our minds unwind to rewind the lines of words that combine

The...

Wishes of yours and the desires of mine

The hours of whine were made to disappear in our rhyme

We're to isolate the signature of our attraction as the greatest sign...

The symbol of unity... and so I spoke of my desires through prayer... Universal Memory...

Allow the scent of her face to permeate my remembrance

Universal Memory...

Allow her illustration to hang in my every frame of mind, let her by my Rembrandt

And...

I won't auction her love for any amount

For all obstacles she surmounts

Her dissertation is picturesque; her speech sets upon a lyrical mount

You're to be...

My happy ending in the flesh, a peaceful walk with the wind

You're to be...

The best period, and our sentence together won't ever end

So memory...

Allow her taste to stay present in my mind's eye

And soul...

Please stay attentive to feel the reaches of her blind sighs

When we're apart...

I know she longs for me as her impatience grows
I'll spin around one hundred globes to drape her spirit with my passionate robe

Understand that you can't escape me, Destiny
For as long as I dream of you, I'll possess this battle's necessary weaponry

I'm fighting for you; I'm fighting to make the sleeping desires true
I'm fighting for you; I'm fighting to make the sleeping desires true

For every day that has ever passed...

You've moved to the rhythm of Earth's tone with thick thighs full of seduction
Eyes full of your husband, words full of substance that enticed me to love you in
massive abundance

Intimately

You run your fingers around my neck as you whisper encouragement for me to
stretch
To last longer and to go deeper until your well of wishes flows in excess

Intimately

Through the curvature of your voluptuous physique, I could tell it would be
angelic
I can smell it and I could never wait to lick it, seal it and male it

I know that you love to be dominant, yet you're submissive to isolated kisses
Let your warming body seep your flavor through your pores and pour out your
vagina's liquid riches

I want it to bathe my tongue; I want to be submerged in your deluge
Know that when your stare asks, "What do you want?" my every atom yells you

I WANT YOU

And...

It's your subtle aggression, you demand my undivided attention
When you please yourself in our exclusivity, I'd be foolish not to lend my
assistance

And...

It's because you hypnotize me with your seduction
Your body language is the symbol signaling me for your abduction

Let me probe you... let me experiment with your mind

For tonight, and every night that has ever passed...

Baby, how I'll deliver it, it'll always be deliberate
I'll only render a tender kiss to your gender's gist, tonight will be honest, and we'll
be innocent

As always...

Slowly my hands wind down the slopes of your oatmeal breasts
I can taste your family's rich lineage when I suck the bend of your arm, your
fingers are out stretched

It's as if...

You're reaching for the future me while I presently take you through the past
I carefully move my mouth toward your explosion and before you explode, I see
my life in a brilliant flash

FLASH!

Flying to last life's vacation destination...

You moaned while your back is against the wall in the public rest room
You screamed, pushed and pulled while going crazy as we explored and trekked
moons

Your physique encouraged me to keep unique with how I reached
I'd require minutes to peel off the clock before I stopped at the depth of your
retreat

FLASH!!

In late November under the Mothership...

We resided in silence; I reclined in and filled inside it in an African bungalow
We chilled in the layers of pleasure as our mist swirled around like jungle snow

We deciphered the tune of harps and lyres, rose upward to a place higher than
higher
We descended for the descendants of Exhaustion but Love dared us to ever tire

And... so we didn't and so we won't

Feel every ribbed vein on my shaft, this length is satisfaction guaranteed
Previously serving as a thermometer, my penile barometer predicts a typhoon will
be heading straight for me

I shall not fear the severe reigns and wins

I stare into your soul as your hands feel around my chest
We roll like rotisserie racks as we're baked by the warmth of Humidity's breath

Sweat forms on my forehead as we turn within the sheets of the bed
They cover us but don't restrict our movement, I'm still held between your legs

It's presents like this that make the future envious and the past regretful
Even now, since I've never met you, you hold a kiss to my lips that'll make it hard
to forget you

How are we doing this?

You've grown with me back to infancy; you'll be the first thing I know
Stay with me until the sands of time cover the fossils of my soul, until memories of
our son don't glow

We've left time and entered Mind; we'd been each other's mine forever now...

For the ones that ask, "Together how?"... we answer...

Infused and glued, imbued from two to infinitely rendezvous
Circumspective views zoomed through jewels clearly see that the bond is true

They'll see us as proof

Motion this picture perfect should be captured and displayed

They'll see us as idols

Though we're nothing to be prayed to; we are the every desire in which one could
pray

They'll see us as moving statues of Love

We're cemented into dimensions of mental visions; impregnating every imagination's womb

They'll see us as comets

Our love making will flame throughout the space of every room

We'll be what it looks like when fire flies... so...

Let our seasoning of love making pepper our memories with marathon memories of mating
Let it be an amazing, blazing creation, allow our insatiable appetite to keep its run pacing

We share an innate endurance for pleasure that's infinite in nature
Who would've ever thought that a timeless and boundless love could be captured within a sheet of paper...

Once again... I didn't... but I will write our love out to the world... and I know you love me to death but...

You love me too much to let me die, yet if I ever did... there would be no way I'd stay dead

I'd haunt you, you'd dream of me, you'd scream from me
You'd cry tears that flow like streams for me, our memories will have you beaming, see...

Because...

You've caressed me on all types of sheets

Every winter

I've made you feel all types of heat

I've...

Role played for you, been all types of he

For forever... I'll be all the types you need

I've whispered sweet somethings in your ears; I've made your femininity tremble and cheer
I'll stay too close to be near, my dear; I'm inside of you here

Don't you hear...

The soft rustle of silk

You grab hold of the surrounding sheets as if to pull them into this experience

Don't you hear...

The soft exhales of my breath

With us inking eternity within the sheets, I've always found that therapeutic for my body's confession

Don't you hear...

The prayers that I still speak

Every utter sent to my unborn children's mother is expressed through my eyes' teary glint

Don't you hear...

The spinning of the world

Time stands no chance in our sexual marathon despite its continuous running; we're not concerned with resting

My kisses to your lips...

They speak of what my stare states, of what my words can't say
Feel me enter you into another dimension of falling time, love making this shocking can faint Space

We'll both allow it to pass out as the waters of your bath splash out

So...

Let my masculine and your feminine trade parts, let the ashes of bedrooms be our trademark
Let's shine bright enough to persuade every jaded heart's midnight desires to never crave the dark

Our submersion in one another...

Is a actualized prophesy that'll be witnessed more emotionally than logically

Our indulgence of each other...

Proves that even ascension to higher intelligence doesn't ease the challenge of this passionate quandary

Should I... enchantingly...

Lumber my timber straight to pass through your tender gate

Continuing to...

Kiss your tender face and astronaut your center space

Or... should I...

Slow the pace and hold your waist, tongue stroll your grace and roll your taste

Continuing to...

Console your faith in how I control the fate of your climax after I hold your quake and have dove in lakes

To shake your mind state and have the trembles massage my face

Decisions... decisions... decisions...

Atop this silken sea of sheets...

Your sunken memoirs of untold pleasures that have been buried all this life now emerge

You authored my devotion for you in secrecy, you encoded the message with Finesse, your treasure keeps my words

Safe... and...

Before sound was created from the music of when our character's mettle hit
Reverberation's rhetoric had already echoed of our passion's etiquette

Know that...

We pour light into the glasses of memory as a courtesy so that all can see a far
sighted vision
I've never meant to be curt to seas but of your personalities, my heart is the only
home for your variety of fishes

And atop this silken sea of sheets...

We swim as mimes, portraying a remembered role from an unlived theatrical
performance
The invitation of your depth is too alluring; my thriving deepening is what your
moans warrant

Baby, hear my thoughts... I question...

Being possessed by your essence, why wouldn't I treat you like my most prized
possession

Not even Reply can answer that question

Enthralled and completely fascinated, our dynamics have been fixated to the eyes
of Obsession

Our status of excellence keeps her questing

You effeminate the Mind in the room

Baby, the seconds always took too long to pass when we've experienced
separation

I've logged forests of feelings within the lined lanes of my notebook's stained
pages
My yearning never ages, yet Time always trades us with others to see how
authentic Love has made us

I remember every time you fell for the fairy tale

When I was Rapunzel

I never told you I held the key to those locked chamber doors

Yet

You still scaled the tower walls despite the height that the dangers soared

I've always loved your persistence... know that

And

There were times where you grew too fond of what your romanticizing vibes provoked
You became an ugly beast while capturing those beauties, and right before the last petal fell from that black rose...

I came... in every life... every time

How dare I ever attempt to sleep while my dream lover walks among nightmares

How dare I...

Not protect my lover's every vulnerability, including his Achilles heel, for those that won't fight fair

I wouldn't... and I haven't... So...

Know that I possess the only love you've known, the only love your spirit will recognize
I have an absolute monopoly over your soul; this type of exactitude could never be jeopardized

And understand...

The qualities, the features, the voice, the hands
The physique, the brain, the mind, the heart of *my* man...

Was engraved in the wind's scroll

Where only the hands of feelings could behold

The heart of my man...

Was encapsulated in the air of even the most grieving of atmospheres
Where the eyeing seconds of Time have come to see that all expect the wiping
away of your tiers

You reign supreme

Your every story of elevation has floored ears to understand...

You reign supreme

Dream's mezzanine has only become so pristine due to the art that you scene

We view that you reign supreme

Your touch precipitates a future of presents and gifts as pleasant as silk showers
wherever your hands land

You reign supreme

Saturn or Venus, ring or no ring, every constellation that's time-bound has
crowned me Queen

I shall not accept less... so...

Let me await the eradication of eternity when I sit on my throne
With you, I'm actually never here so I've adopted reality as our own...

Image of interpretation... every reel is real

The downpour of rain picks up outside

Lightning streaks and thunder crackles as our positions move backward

You impress me; the mattress fits a silk mouthpiece to muffle my screams
I passionately push against the headboard as if it's the door that'll lead me back to
the room I'm currently realizing my dream

I'd travel back up the stairs that'll lead me back to the exact spot I'm in now

To again witness our...

Heavenly ebony textures wave in the wake that this sex surfs
I embrace the way we skate and my heart heats like I'm wearing a million sweat shirts

I can relive our lives of love making forever

But...

For the strength of your hands to grip my hips and waist
For your breath to outline and trace my grace and your lips to kiss and taste...

I'd wait another life time

For the chance to romance in France
For the taking off of clothes that never land and for the moment we buy time to share and...

Engage in world shattering love making... I'd wait another 10 lives

Because I push against this headboard like it's a door to the past...

Know that if this union was to ever cease...

I'd decay from the withering height of a thousand stories of depression
I'd vacation in Melancholic's tropic where I'd confide in grey skies with all of my confessions

I'd...

Tear fire from eyes of flames with a burning heart that was filled with despair and shame
I'd forever deny my secret garden the pleasure of a meatier shower; I'll be Sahara to another reign

I'd...

Fall into a slumber and wish to never awaken again if it's not to your smile
I'd snore forever more and only dream of adopting every sun as our child

I'd...

Deal with Silence's abuse in recluse as my eyes close to review everything I knew
of you

And I'd...

Live mad, deliriously in denial that each schizophrenic stint is proof that your
absence isn't true

We've never been truly apart... We're never truly apart... We'll never truly be apart

So believe that...

This red hot bed homes dreadlocked legs of cycling passion
Time sights our flight of flying as matching, this night is forever flashing

And for those millions of miles away... we are the stars that shine

Across the surface of the worlds without air, we have still breathed life in it
We've kept careful and exact detail of our accounts so that anyone could relive
our minutes

And know of Love.... And because of my love for you...

I'll be light as a rock and use your body for my basking
I'll reside in your veins and paint the liquid the hue of passion

In retrospect you'll see me as...

Your only lover, your past's oldest, brightest burning flicker of the oldest flame
I was destined and born to be 'Her' and no one but me shall hold this claim

Know that as I thrust back into your abs, I'm giving it all back...

All of the spices and sugars that are in me...

I'm giving them to you

All of the techniques and movements that Jealousy has envied...

I'm giving them to you

I bend and twist my back's arch like a bow tie...

Sweetly... glazed

I bend dips and my swoops sweep low and high

See me engaged

My mahogany mystery has only been for you to solve
For you to have its all, to answer it call and for your penis to furnish its eternal hall

So whether my exterior walls are of oatmeal, honey, beige, caramel, or copper...

The medley of my fruit's melody is composed for you to master its song

And

My body's coffee canvas is yours to stir and hop butterscotch tongues upon

So...

Navigate my labyrinth of enigmas with certainty

You constructed the design of my maze

I wrap around you with the entire worth of me

My imagination has constructed the confines of your daze

Looking back at you from over my shoulder I want you to know that...

I've taken pleasure in holding hands with the universe and being the reason responsible for turning it
I've taken pleasure every second we celebrated ancient anniversaries in heavens of angelic furnishings

Because in the house of Love

We've dined under the pure light of diamond chandeliers
Our burning stares produced waxed memories when the temperature cooled
from our candle tears

We've entertained and slow danced across many gold trimmed glass floors
We've worn garments of the finest fabrics while spinning within a time that passed
slower

For years and years, year after year

Beds had become...

Stages showing the aerial acts of my legs and choreography of our souls
Coliseums and museums where we've shown freedom rests in every touch we
hold

For years and years, year after year

Beds had become...

Oceans where I were mermaids with fins of feathers made of ruby medley
Our heart's home as the start of every day reminded me to be gracious of the day
you met me

I love you

To hear my sole's whispers, continue to hold my ankles by your ears
I'll be sure to speak expressively and descriptively, I want the pictures to be clear

And in the House of Love

You explained that what you feel is timeless and that nothing would change your
vision of me
Our ancestral tree is rooted in your belief; you're the type of man that every
woman truly seeks

For as long as long is...

I want your heart and soul, your body and your mind

I want you for as long as

The sun floats in the sky

And

The stars sparkle up high

I want you for as long as

Autumn leaves her fleeing presence for the ground

And

Elliptical axes keep the galaxy's planets spinning around

I want you for as long as

March's troops spring forth with revelations of coming glory

And

Thorn-less stems of roses stir Love's thoughts of amore'

I want you for as long as

Thirsty oceans lap at the moist sands of the beach

And

Patient cacti stick out the cold nights for the return of the desert's heat

I want you for as long as I know you exist... I want you for forever

You swing your legs from your kneeling position so they sit along side me
Your grasp shifts the tides in me, it says, "Come ride with me"

So I spin around

I can feel the orgasm whirling; it's twirling from deep within me
Feelings rush through my mind as rapidly as white watered twin seas

You hold my waist as...

I rock your strong shaft against my cream slickened walls
The strength of your pillar slows my rhythmic swaying to a stiffening crawl

My God, you're completely submerged

The rain's fall has reached its most relentless dance
You read my body language and can see that the course of Nature's plans...

Won't be denied

You resume presence in my mind, you declare

I want you to feel my entire thrusting from beneath thee, I'm gritting my teeth
I can feel the pulse of your heart beat with my reach; immense light is all I see

The time is nearing, what we've been awaiting is tired of waiting
Within the night our dawn shall awaken, I can feel your legs shaking

I lean up and place my hands to your throat

You grab my wrists for leverage as you regain your momentum
The passion and pleasures I impale your body with, Soul sent them

And

I see it happening, I see your eyes start to roll back
I, too, no longer hold back, any preceding impurities are receding into the black...

Into the black of Forgotten

Your grip breaks the skin on my wrists; you slam your nails into my chest
I release my hands from your neck as you come down to let your lips rest...

Along my collar bone and chin... along my lips and face

I grip your butt and release the recipe of creation into your melting pot
You exhale in my ear as my geyser's shooting force rains ecstasy throughout your loving lot

Heavy panting accompanied by exhaustion finally brings a halt to our night
I know we've used all of our might; I kiss you lazily as I know we've done
everything right

And now it all makes sense... I remember

She breathed a speech that whispered the guarantee of everything I would seek
Her body language leaked a majestic message every time her persistent inhibitions
would cease

You're "Her"

You've needed me inside of your mind, your dreams, throughout time
My tongue tied actions would unwind whenever your unraveling soul would be
kind

You ran sprints of touches over my chest, marathons of stares came with your
caress
When my turn came to decode her body of text, no purple blushing night would
come to see me rest

I was destined and ordained to...

Arrange your limbs into my grasp as if they were the strangest gems
Our passion out ranges sin, my finger's breast stroke insinuates that I indeed came
to swim

I cover you, my lips water her, my carnivorous passion waits to slaughter her
You gave your life to finding a love worth dying for; you're an angel second,
martyr first

I scaled the Walls of Perfection with a confident affection
Your hips gave direction; my interjection with an erection didn't interrupt the
session

For centuries... I made your eyes roll back

The stories Love bought of inferior lovers were sold back
Pressing climaxes made you fold back, pure and explicit ecstasy, you were owed
that

I mouthed the spout of rejuvenation, our hearts resumed their racing
What we shared was intimate; it was a simple yet deep conversation

And

You breathed a speech that whispered the guarantee of everything I would seek
Your body language leaked a majestic message, may our inhibitions forever stay
deceased

You open your eyes and look to me... we speak

I love you
I love you

Stéphane Parker is currently working on Eternal Wish which is the last part of this Eternal Love Trilogy.

Champagne Dreams, which is the story behind the eternal lovers depicted throughout the trilogy, is currently in its first stages of rough draft.

Find Stéphane Parker on Facebook and become a fan of the Passion.

www.ParkerRomance.com

Grandma Dot, I love you.

www.ingramcontent.com/pod-product-compliance
Lightning Source LLC
Chambersburg PA
CBHW030637130626
46552CB00002B/901